DARE

A MEN OF INKED HEATWAVE NOVEL

www.chellebliss.com

CHELLE BLISS

USA TODAY BESTSELLING AUTHOR

MEN OF INKED: HEATWAVE SERIES

Book 1 - Flame

Book 2 - Burn

Book 3 - Wildfire

Book 4 - Blaze

Book 5 - Ignite

Book 6 - Spark

Book 7 - Ember

Book 8 - Singe

Book 9 - Ashes

Book 10 - Scorch

Book 11 - Torch

Book 12 - Inferno

Book 13 - Cinder

Book 14 - Dare

To learn more,
please visit *menofinked.com/heatwave-series*

BE A GALLO GIRL...

Want to be the first to hear about the next Men of Inked book or everything Chelle Bliss? Join my newsletter by _tapping here to sign up_ or visit _menofinked.com/inked-news_

Want a place to talk romance books, meet other bookworms, and all things Men of Inked? Join Chelle Bliss Books on Facebook to get sneak peeks, exclusive news, and special giveaways.

COPYRIGHT @ 2024 BLISS INK

Publisher © Chelle Bliss January 30th 2024
Edited by Lisa A. Hollett
Proofread by Read By Rose & Shelley Carlton
Cover Design © Chelle Bliss
Cover Photo © Eric Battershell Photography
Cover Model: Frank Alesci

www.chellebliss.com

CHELLE BLISS

USA TODAY BESTSELLING AUTHOR

CHAPTER 1
SAGE

NINETEEN YEARS UNDER MY PARENTS' roof, four mediocre years studying history in college, months at boot camp, and then A school had me craving freedom and fun.

"Are you settled in?" my dad asked as I walked out of my building.

"Totally settled." I glanced around, watching as hordes of people headed toward the mess hall.

"Allison there?"

"She's somewhere, but I was just heading to dinner," I lied, knowing I was going the opposite direction.

"When in doubt, always go for the salad. It's the least likely thing to kill you."

"Got it." I tucked my hand into the pocket of my coat, fishing out my car keys. "Trust me, Dad. I've memorized everything you told me."

He sighed on the other end of the phone. "I should've pulled some strings and had you stationed closer."

"I have to do this on my own," I told him, stalking toward the crowded parking lot. "I *want* to do this on my own. Promise me you won't get involved, Kasper?" I used his call sign, something I'd heard him called a million times by his friends.

"I won't, sunshine. I swear."

"I'm in no way a ray of sunshine, Daddy. Maybe to you, but no one else."

"Got a nickname yet? Chaos would be a great one for you."

I chuckled, knowing he was right. I was like a ball of chaos, too wild to be caged, too unwieldy to be anything else. "Nope," I lied again. "Just Sage or Hill. You know how it is when you're new."

"You'll find your place, sweetheart. When's duty start?"

"I have a few days to settle in."

"Everything is hurry up and wait. I'd like to say it gets better, but it doesn't." My dad loved talking about the navy. He wasn't just a regular sailor. Nope. My dad was the elite. The crème de la crème. A navy SEAL through and through.

I had no plans to break the proverbial glass ceiling, trying to be one of the first female SEALs ever. I was happy to find my place as a quartermaster without the pressure of saving lives and risking my own on a daily basis.

"Hill." Blondie, my best friend from boot camp, waved across the parking lot, leaning against my car. "Get your ass moving. We're losin' daylight."

"I've got to go, Dad. I'm here. I'm safe. I'm ready."

"Okay. Okay. I'm so proud of you. You know that, right?"

"I do." I waved back at Blondie when he didn't stop glaring at me because I wasn't moving fast enough. "I love you, Daddy."

"Love you too. Give 'em hell."

"That's the plan. I'll call soon."

"Tomorrow?" he asked.

"I'll text you tomorrow."

"Fuck," he grumbled. "A text is fine."

"Go spend time with Mom or Sawyer, Dad. I'm heading to the world-famous salad bar you've been raving about for years," I said sarcastically.

Dad chuckled. "Later, kid."

"Bye, Dad."

"Well, Jesus. If you move any slower, we'll get there tomorrow," Blondie said as I jammed my phone into the back pocket of my jeans.

"What's the hurry? It's not even five."

Blondie ran his hand over his cropped brown hair, always looking exasperated. "It's our first night without curfew, and I'm not wasting it."

If Blondie and I hadn't become best friends at A school, I'd find him attractive. But there was something about him that made him feel more like my brother than possible boyfriend material. His blue eyes and full lips made most of the girls swoon, but I just didn't see him the same way.

I clicked to open the locks to my Jeep, wanting nothing more than some time off base. "Where are we going anyway?"

He settled into the passenger seat, looking like a giant folded up, with his knees almost touching his chest. "I found the perfect spot down by the ocean."

"It's the Gulf, not the ocean," I corrected, sliding the key into the ignition.

"Um, it's still an ocean."

I glanced over at him, unable to keep the judgment from my face. "Listen, the Atlantic is the ocean. The Gulf is the…"

"Gulf?" he teased. "It's still endless blue water, babe."

"You're a goofball."

"You try growing up in a cornfield in Indiana. I'm sorry I wasn't a spoiled little girl from Virginia where the ocean was in my backyard."

I backed out, ignoring his comment. "Where am I going?"

"The Rusty Knuckle."

I gaped at him as I shifted my Jeep into drive,

keeping my foot firmly planted on the brake. "The what?"

"Rusty Knuckle. Supposed to be the hottest bar on the beach."

"Sounds like it." I laughed. "Why there? I heard the Seagull is so much better."

Blondie blanched and pulled on his tank top, the same one he always wore because it showed off his muscles. "Because the Seagull isn't a biker bar."

"Biker bar?" A car honked behind us when I didn't move, still gawking at my dumb friend. "Why the hell are we going to a biker bar?"

"Nothing sexier than a woman in leather," Blondie said, as if we were having a normal conversation, which we weren't. "Find the gas, babe, and hit it."

A few minutes of silence passed as we drove off base, heading toward the water. "So, leather, huh?" I asked curiously. I'd always pegged him as the type to fall for someone a bit more like Little Bo Peep than Joan Jett.

Blondie turned up the radio, blasting an old heavy metal tune, moving his head like he was in a classic rock band. "Nothing sexier."

"You're a freak." I laughed, tapping my thumb against the steering wheel, following the beat of the music. "I think that's why we're friends."

"We were meant to be together."

I glanced at him, curling my lip. "Not happening."

"I know. I know." He lifted his hands. "I mean we were meant to be friends, Hill. You're a freak like me. You hide it so much better, but I could see it the moment I laid eyes on you."

"You have freak-dar."

He nodded, studying my profile as I drove. "Why do you hide it, anyway?"

"You met my parents at graduation, Blondie. Enough said, no?"

"They seemed really sweet."

"Sweet? Are you serious?"

"They were sweet. And how would I know otherwise? You barely talk about them. Your mom looks like she's a runway model, and your dad looked like he was a badass at some point."

I laughed louder. "When they visit, I want you to recite that statement in front of him."

"I may be young, but I'm not stupid. And he may be old, but he could probably still beat my ass to a pulp."

"With one arm tied behind his back."

"So, tell me, what's their story?" he asked, angling his body so he was facing me and turning down the volume on the radio.

"You can't tell anyone. Promise me," I begged.

"I promise," he said, but his tone was not convincing.

I glared at him for a moment. "I mean it, Blondie. You can't tell anyone."

"Are they felons? On the run from the Feds? Come on, Hill. Now, you have to tell me about them."

I didn't answer, keeping my eyes on the road.

"Fine. Fine. I promise I won't tell anyone, and if I do, you can cut off my nads and shove them down my throat."

I winced, picturing the entire scene. "That's a little much, but I would beat the shit out of you."

"Like to see you try. Now, talk."

"Bossy fucker," I muttered. "Why do I always surround myself with impossible men?"

"You need the strength around you to calm the chaos."

"I wasn't asking your opinion," I told him, rolling my eyes after being called chaos for a second time today.

"Then don't ask the question out loud."

I groaned, hating him for a minute for being impossible like almost everyone else in my life.

"Helloooo," Blondie said. "Tell me about your parents."

"Tell me about yours first," I shot back, wanting to know about his life before I told him about mine.

"My mom is an elementary art teacher, and my dad is a farmer. Corn, remember?"

I nodded, liking that his parents led normal lives. I was actually jealous he never had to worry about his parents dying on the job. "Sounds like a nice life."

"It was boring, and I don't plan to end up like them."

"There're worse things to be."

"Maybe, Hill, maybe. Now spill the beans on beauty and the beast."

"Beauty and the beast?" I smirked.

"Your mom and pop. Who are they?"

"Fine." I sighed. "My mom worked for the FBI, and so did her brothers and father. It's a family tradition, but one I plan to break. Dad, well, he was a SEAL before he retired and now spends more time building birdhouses than saving the world." There was not a word from Blondie after I finished speaking, and I turned, wondering if he was still alive. "What?" I asked when I saw the pinched expression on his face.

"FBI and a SEAL? Seriously?"

I nodded and shrugged. "Uh, yeah. Seriously."

"Jesus. Wow."

"Not Jesus. Just soldiers."

Blondie laughed, slapping his legs. "Your mom was G.I. Jane and your dad was G.I. Joe, and you're saying they were just soldiers."

"G.I. Jane wasn't in the FBI."

"There it is." Blondie pointed out the window, and my eyes followed.

I pointed at the dive bar with a row of motorcycles. "You want to go there?"

"You a pussy now?" he teased.

I lifted my chin. "Never been a pussy a day in my life."

"Of course not, G.I. Junior."

I pulled into an empty parking spot and glared at him as I put the Jeep in park. "I am not G.I. Junior."

An easy, playful smile spread across his face. "You so are."

"Whatever."

Blondie climbed down from the Jeep, stretching like we'd driven for longer than five minutes. "I'm ready to get a little wild. How about you?"

"I was born wild," I told him, throwing him a wink.

"I have no doubt." He stalked toward the front doors, cracking his neck. "Once we're inside, we're going separate ways."

I gawked at him and stopped walking. "You're ditching me?"

"Well, yeah. How am I supposed to get laid with a girl next to me? I came here to get laid, not hang out."

"What the hell am I supposed to do?"

Blondie ticked his head toward the run-down building. "I don't know... Maybe find someone and get yourself laid too."

I wrinkled my nose and threw my arm out toward the place. "At a biker bar?"

"There's no better place to find a piece of ass with no strings attached. No one's here for forever."

My lip curled as I strode past him and headed to the door. "We're not friends anymore."

He ran up next to me, slowing when our shoulders were side by side. "Liar…you love me."

I looked him up and down, snarling. "You can go screw yourself. I'm hungry. I'm grabbing a burger and a soda and heading back to base. You can find your own way back."

"I wasn't planning on going back with you. I'm going to get my dick sucked at the very least, maybe twice if it's a good night."

"You're disgusting."

He shrugged, grabbing the door handle before I could as if he was a gentleman. "I'm a man."

"You're an idiot," I told him before walking inside and heading straight to an empty chair at the bar.

"Later, Hill," Blondie called out somewhere behind me, but I barely heard him over the chatter and music.

"Fucker," I muttered, sliding onto a stool.

"What'll it be?" a man with the biggest beer belly I'd ever seen asked me.

"A menu and a Coke."

"A Coke?" He blinked, his bushy white eyebrows twitching.

"A Coke," I growled.

He threw his hands up and backed away.

"Fuckin' right," I said to myself. "You better move along."

A man laughed. "That was one of the funniest damn things I've ever seen."

I ignored him, not knowing if he was talking to me and not caring even if he was. I just kept tapping my fingers against the sticky bar top, hating Blondie and men in general.

"Put whatever she wants on my tab," the man next to me said to the bartender as he slid the glass of Coke in front of me, followed by a menu.

"I'm perfectly fine paying for my own drink," I told the guy, not glancing at him but glaring at the bartender who looked at me like I was vicious and bitchy.

"Whatever she wants, she gets," the bartender replied.

"It takes a lot to rattle Clive, but somehow, you did it. All five foot three inches of you."

"Five four," I corrected him, eyeing the appetizer section as soon as I flipped open the menu.

I could feel the weight of his stare, even with my eyes glued to the endless list of things I wanted to eat. After eating military food for months, every time I was able to eat at a real restaurant, even a dive bar, it was a treat.

"You got a problem?" I asked, annoyed by the way he was staring.

"No problem at all, darlin'. Just trying to figure

out how you stay upright with that giant chip you're carrying on your shoulder."

I set the menu down, placing my hand on top of the greasy plastic before I swiveled around on my stool, coming eye-to-eye with the man who felt the need to speak to me. "Excuse me?" I asked, my voice filled with venom.

The corner of his lip tipped up. "You heard me," he said, looking all adorable with his cropped dark hair, strong jaw, and icy blue eyes. "Doesn't it get exhausting acting so tough all the time?"

I twisted my lips and curled my hand into a ball as I did everything I could to hold myself back from socking him in his handsome face. "How hard is it for you to be a constant asshole all the time? I mean, eventually, you have to get sick of your own shit."

He chuckled, running his hand across his trimmed beard. "You're as funny as you are beautiful."

"Gee, thanks," I snapped. "My entire day has been made by your compliment."

I needed to get out of the bar, away from this guy. He screamed trouble. The type of man you could tell left broken hearts wherever he went. Just the type I'd fall for and then become another casualty in his past.

"What branch?" he asked out of nowhere as if I had a neon sign above my head that flashed "Military."

"None of your business." I tore my eyes away from him and took a five from my pocket.

I was so pissed at Blondie for ditching me, and I was taking it out on the man next to me, who had done nothing wrong besides giving me a compliment. But I knew better. Nothing good happened in places like this. The last thing I needed right now was to hook up with a stranger and end up with an STI as a parting gift for my stupidity.

"Where you running off to?" the handsome man asked as I threw the money on the bar.

"This isn't my scene," I told him, climbing to my feet. "And you aren't my type."

"I'm everybody's type, darlin'," he said, smirking.

Ugh. He was too.

There wasn't a thing about him someone in the world wouldn't find attractive. From his good looks, toned biceps, and probably muscular-everywhere-else body, his dreamy blue eyes, the sexy-as-hell smirk…the man could probably bed any woman he wanted.

"I'm all about confidence, buddy, but you're a little much even for me," I lied.

"Austin," he stated.

"Austin?"

He nodded. "Name isn't buddy. It's Austin."

"Good to know," I told him before walking away, heading toward the parking lot.

"Hey, sweet cheeks, want a ride?" a man said as soon as I stepped outside.

I kept walking, not bothering to stop and tell him

to fuck off. Now wasn't the time, and this wasn't the place.

I continued to ignore the catcalls and whistles from various men as I made my way to my Jeep, climbing inside and slamming the door. I sighed, resting my head against the steering wheel for a few seconds, letting myself cool off before I tried to drive away.

When I was angry, I usually had a lead foot. The last thing I needed right now was another ticket. Two deep breaths later, I lifted my head, placed the key in the ignition, and twisted.

But instead of turning on, the Jeep made the most horrendous sound, like the engine was grinding and nothing else.

"Goddamn it!" I shouted to myself, slamming my palms against the steering wheel. "Not again, you bastard."

I leaned back, resting my head against the seat, and closed my eyes. I'd give it a few minutes, trying not to flood the engine before I tried to start the Jeep again.

I jumped at the tap on my window, and my eyes flew open, my head twisting to the side. "Fucking hell," I muttered, clutching my chest and breathing heavy.

"You need help?" Austin, the hot, cocky bastard from inside the bar, asked.

I rolled down the window because my Jeep was

old and didn't have fancy electric windows. "I'm fine. Move along."

He laughed, lifting his forearm to rest it against the doorframe. "I'm not leaving until you get her running."

"It's a he and he's a little volatile, but he'll run smooth after he warms up a little."

"He sounds just like his owner."

I rolled my eyes, turning my head away from Austin to stare out the windshield. Maybe if I ignored him, refused to engage with him, he'd leave. It was possible, and if all else failed, I'd pull out my big guns and chase him away.

A minute later, with me still staring out the front window, ignoring him, he pushed off the car. I let out a breath, knowing victory was mine and he was finally leaving me alone. But then he turned, his ass moving to the passenger door as he crossed his arms over his chest, staring out across the parking lot.

"What are you doing?" I asked, watching him in my side mirror, my eyes wandering down his muscular frame.

"I'm not leaving you alone in a place like this with a car that isn't working."

"I don't need to be rescued."

"I'm just here as backup."

"Don't need that either."

"Try it again," he ordered, turning his head to stare at me.

"What?" I narrowed my gaze, still looking at him in the side mirror, neither of us moving or backing down.

"The engine. Try it again."

I growled, cursing under my breath and praying the Jeep's engine would start this time. If it didn't, I had a feeling Austin was going to make me his mission.

And because sometimes the universe was cruel and unforgiving, when I turned the key, absolutely nothing happened.

Fuck.

CHAPTER 2
AUSTIN

THERE WERE GIRLS, and then there were women. The one inside her Jeep, throwing a fit, was most certainly a woman, but acted like a little girl. She was pissed and rightfully so, but for some reason, she was taking it out on me.

No one ever wanted to be rescued. Not unless it was life or death. We all liked to think we were self-sustaining, able to care for ourselves, but sometimes it was nice to have a helping hand.

"So, darlin', looks like you need a ride," I told her as soon as she turned the key, and the Jeep didn't even try to turn over. "Where ya headed?"

She wrinkled her nose. "Just give me a jump, and we can go our separate ways."

I shook my head and pushed off the car, stepping back to her window. "Although the idea of jumping you sounds fantastic, I can't. I only have my bike with me."

She grabbed her phone from the center console, tapping on the screen like the thing was to blame for her problems. "Fine," she grunted. "I'll just call roadside assistance."

"I'll wait with you, then."

She snapped her head to the side as she dropped her phone in her lap. "You're staying?"

I nodded.

"Why?"

I leaned against her window, careful not to put my face too close. This one was a wild thing, and she was liable to bite. "I wasn't raised to leave a woman alone in a place like this. My grandmother would whip my ass if she ever found out. So, I'm staying. Once roadside is here and your Jeep is running, I'll go."

She grunted again, resting her head on the back of the seat, and stared up at the roof of the Jeep. "You have no idea how self-sufficient I really am."

I shook my head. "Don't know and don't care. I was raised old-school, and I stayed old-school. There're some ways things should go, and a man staying with a stranded woman is one of them."

"Austin, right?" she asked.

I smiled, liking she remembered my name. "Yeah, darlin'. Austin. And you are?"

"My friends call me Hill."

"Hill," I muttered. "Want to wait inside for them

to come? I'll buy you something to eat and another Coke?"

She wrinkled her nose as her stomach rumbled, liking my idea too.

"Beats sitting out here waiting."

Her gaze swept across my face as if she was trying to decide whether I was trustworthy. "I'll go inside with you only because it's safer than being outside with you."

I smiled. "Works for me," I said, peeling myself off from her truck and backing away.

"Hello," she said into the phone. "My car won't start, and I'm in need of assistance." She rolled up the window, leaving me outside and not privy to the rest of the conversation.

I stood outside, a few feet away, checking my phone instead of staring at her. When her Jeep door opened and she climbed down, I finally looked up again. "All set?"

She nodded. "They'll be here in about an hour."

"Perfect amount of time to grab some grub," I told her, tucking my phone back into my pocket.

"I can eat alone."

"Jesus. Are you always this stubborn?" I lifted my hands, exasperated by this woman.

She raised her chin as she slammed the door to her Jeep. "Being stubborn isn't always a negative." She turned to face me, eyes narrowed and attitude firmly in place. "And for your information, I'm not stubborn. I'm cautious. They're two very different things." She stalked toward the bar, leaving me standing there, gawking at her.

Why I didn't walk away, I had no idea. Usually, I would. I'd never had to try this hard with anyone before.

But I didn't stand there for long before I ran up next to her, grabbing the door handle before she could. "If I wanted to do you harm, I would've done it when we were alone out there." I ticked my head toward the parking lot where her yellow Jeep was parked.

She stared at me for a moment as I held open the door, her green eyes blazing. "I can still be cautious. Maybe you're trying to get me to let my guard down."

"In you go, darlin'." I pushed her back softly, nudging her inside the bar, instead of standing outside having this ridiculous conversation.

The move earned me a look of death, but she kept walking straight to the bar and the two seats we'd been sitting in before. "You know I could break your arm without breaking a sweat," she told me as she slid onto the stool and crossed her legs in the most ladylike way.

I raised an eyebrow, laughing softly as I sat down next to her. "You think?"

"Yeah."

"You're almost a foot shorter than me and less

than half my weight. While it might be possible, Hill, I highly doubt you have the ability."

An easy smile spread across her face. "Maybe you're the one who should be cautious of me, Austin."

I laughed louder, motioning for the bartender from earlier. "Coke for the lady, and I'll take a Jack and Coke," I said to him when he came near.

"Maybe I wanted something stronger," she said.

"Do you?"

"No."

"Impossible woman," I muttered.

"Hill," a guy said, coming up behind her, throwing his arm over her shoulder. "This is Betty."

The dark-haired woman under his arm blushed. "It's Belinda," she corrected him, but she didn't seem too fazed.

"Found a piece of ass that quick, Blondie?" Hill curled her lip at the bimbo plastered against his side.

"Look at you," he said, swinging his eyes from her to me. "You worked quick too. I knew you had it in you, tiger."

"Fuck off, Blondie," she snarled, shrugging off his arm.

"Gladly," he said with a grin on his face as he moved back into the crowd with the girl on his arm.

"Friend of yours?"

She turned around, finding the Coke the bartender had set in front of her while her friend stopped by to say hello. "We were until tonight."

"Why didn't you tell him about the Jeep?" I asked, knowing she could've gotten rid of me if he would've stayed.

She shrugged. "He's here for one thing, and it isn't helping me."

"I'm sure he would've ditched the chick for you."

She shook her head. "He wouldn't. He made that much clear when he invited me out tonight and then left me before we made it to the front door. I thought we were coming here to unwind, have a few drinks, but then he took off and told me he needed to get laid."

So, her words told me a few things. One, Blondie was not a threat in any way. She didn't like him sexually or romantically. Second, she had shitty friends. And last, she needed to unwind, which I already knew because if she was wound any tighter, she'd snap.

"Been friends for long?" I asked because she'd suddenly stopped talking, and I wasn't going to let the chance to find out more pass.

"Just a few months." She placed the straw between her lips, sipping her drink, looking everywhere but at me.

"He new to town, or are you?"

She stared at me out of the corner of her eye. "Both of us are...were. You?"

"I'm only here for a few weeks," I told her, finally reaching for my drink.

"Vacation?"

"Work." I lifted my filled glass toward her. "To new friends…"

She wrinkled her nose. "They're not all they're cracked up to be." Hill turned her head, waving down the bartender. "Do you know what you want to order?" she asked me as he stalked our way. "I'm starving."

"I'll have my usual."

She glared at me, eyes narrowing. "How can you have a usual if you're only passing through?"

"I was stationed here for a bit and used to live here, but now I'm on the West Coast in California."

"Navy?" She quirked an eyebrow.

I nodded.

"What'll it be?" Clive, the bartender who'd probably worked here since opening day, asked us.

"Cheeseburger and fries," Hill told him, pushing the menu she'd barely looked at in his direction.

"Same."

Clive gave me a look, raising one bushy eyebrow. He wanted to say something. I could practically see the words hanging on the tip of his tongue, but he only shook his head and walked away.

"Where are you from originally? You have an accent."

"It's a long story."

She sighed. "We have nothing but time, Ace."

"Ace?" I laughed.

She shrugged. "I'm sure you have some cute little nickname."

I grumbled because I did not have a cute little nickname. Mine was ridiculous, and I hated anyone outside my inner circle knowing it. "No nickname," I lied, staring at the bar because lying to her sweet face seemed wrong.

"Liar," she replied, bumping me with her shoulder. "Come on. Tell me what it is."

I turned my head and lifted an eyebrow. "What's yours?"

"Hill." She shrugged. "Nothing interesting or funny."

"Hill…because?" I asked as Clive placed our burgers in front of us.

"I'm built like a mountain." She smiled, winking at me.

I tilted my head, eyeing her and the ridiculousness. "You're shitting me."

She giggled. "Totally shitting you." She grabbed another fry, placing it on her lip, but held it there. "My last name is Hill."

"And your first name?"

She sighs. "Sage."

"Sage," I repeated, smiling because the unusual name fit her.

"I know, it's boring. Now, tell me your nickname."

"Han Solo," I answered honestly and went back

to staring at my plate instead of her. "Stupid nickname."

"Hmm," she hummed next to me, a smirk firmly planted on her pouty lips. "Let me think." She tapped her bottom lip, taunting me. "Nicknames always have meaning."

"Drop it," I told her, pushing her plate closer to her. "You don't want your fries to get cold."

"You're wicked with a sword?" She raised an eyebrow.

I shook my head as I grabbed my burger and took a big bite.

She studied me for a moment, her eyes roaming my face. "Han Solo," she whispered so softly, I barely heard her.

She was cute in that moment.

A side of her I hadn't seen since the second I'd laid eyes on her. There was a hardness to her, a toughness most women didn't have, no matter how hard the military tried to drill it into them. But Sage, she was different. She had been raised differently, and without knowing a damn thing about her parents, I knew someone had to be military.

The navy had given me discipline. Something I'd been lacking most of my life. I could easily spot a military brat from a civilian after just a few words. They carried themselves differently.

"Did you get caught jackin' off or something?" she asked.

The cheeseburger that had started its journey down my throat became lodged. I choked, pounding on my chest, trying to force the dry-ass piece of beef to move down and allow me to breathe again.

"Oh. My. God." She laughed, covering her mouth. "You got caught, and that's why they call you Han Solo." She made a motion with her hand like she was stroking a cock.

None of which made swallowing, breathing, or not losing my shit any easier. "Fuck no," I choked out between gasps, pounding harder on my chest to the point I was going to leave a bruise.

"You so fucking did," she argued, still laughing at my misery.

"Stop." I held up my hand, needing her to stop so I could catch my breath. "That's not what happened."

She crossed her arms, lifting her chin with a twinkle in her eyes. "Then tell me, because right now, I'm sticking with my hypothesis."

I cleared my throat, buying time and hoping something else would happen to get us off the topic of my nickname. I'd always hated it. It was stupid and embarrassing, but nowhere near as bad as being caught masturbating as she'd assumed.

"So," I said, coughing once more when no rescue came. "It was right after A school, and my girlfriend had moved near the base to be closer to me."

Hill rolled her eyes. "Weak," she muttered.

I held up a finger. "We'd dated on and off for

about six months, and I didn't think we were that serious. But she thought otherwise and followed me."

The single sentence earned me a gag from Sage. "I mean, you're not bad-looking, but…"

I narrowed my eyes and continued. "Anyway, I was out with my friends, having a few beers, kind of like tonight."

"We're not friends."

"I know," I growled, throwing up my hand. "You want to hear this or not?"

She grabbed another fry and held it up, waving the long stick in the air. "I seriously like my explanation better. So, if you don't want to continue, you can stop now."

I shoved her arm, moving the fry toward her lips. "Eat and be quiet for two goddamn minutes."

"I hit a chord with someone." She giggled but finally relented, placing the food in her mouth, giving me a moment of silence.

"Sissy comes storming into the bar." I glanced around, realizing the main event happened right here in almost the same exact spot.

"Wait," Sage said, clutching her chest with that damn smirk back on her lips. "You dated a chick named Sissy?"

I nodded.

"Sissy? That's really someone's name? It has to be short for something."

"She's a Southern woman. It's a common nickname."

"What's her real name?"

"Cecilia."

"Go on," she said, waving her hand at me before she propped her chin against her palm, elbow on the bar. "Tell me all about Sissy and Han Solo. I'm intrigued."

I washed down her sarcasm with the Jack and Coke, staring her down. "She stormed into the bar, screaming at me in front of everyone about how I was a shitty boyfriend and how I better get used to my hand because I'd never sleep with her again."

"Sounds like a lovely human."

I shrugged, remembering a time when Sissy wasn't off her rocker. "She had her moments."

Sage batted her eyelashes. "I'm sure you were with her for her kind heart and not her what I'd assume were big breasts."

My hand moved to my neck, rubbing the spot she'd made tense up. The girl was good at getting under people's skin. She reminded me of an interrogator, always trying to throw the other person off, which she was doing with flying colors. "I'm more of an ass man, Hill," I teased, winking at her, hoping to get under her skin now.

She turned her head for a moment, but not before I saw the red flush creep across her cheeks. "Why were you a shitty boyfriend?"

She might be busting my balls, throwing me tons of attitude, pretending she didn't like me even as a friend, but she was into me. Nothing that came out of her mouth going forward would change my mind.

I kneaded deeper into the muscles near my shoulder, thinking about Sissy and her antics, especially at the end. "She said I was supposed to be at home with her, watching the *Gilmore Girls*." I gagged, shaking off the memories of all the girlie shit.

"I loved that show."

I raised an eyebrow, gawking at this chick who, while feminine, wasn't girlie.

Sage snorted. "Just fucking with you." She touched my arm, blushing again when my gaze dipped to where our bodies were connected. She snatched her hand back so quickly, as if the contact was enough to burn her flesh. "My mom loved that show," she laughed, acting as if whatever moment we'd just had never happened. "Which, if you knew my mother, you'd know how absurd that statement really is."

"Your mom a lot like you, then?"

She tilted her head, all playfulness gone. "Like me?"

I lifted my chin, smirking. "You're a tough chick, Hill."

"First—" she put up a finger so close to my face, I couldn't focus on the single digit "—I'm not a chick. I'm a woman."

"Yep," I said, my gaze dipping, taking her all in. "Noticed that as soon as I saw you."

Her finger moved to my chin, forcing my eyes upward. "Second, I have to be tough. There's no room for weakness in today's world and definitely not in the military—especially if you're a woman."

"You can't be hard all the time, darlin'."

"Darlin'?" she snorted. "You Southern boys and your charm."

"Would you rather I call you dumplin'?"

"Hill or Sage. Definitely not dumplin'."

"Sure, darlin'," I said, aggravating her more. But I liked her this way. I loved the fire in her eyes and the spark I saw inside her.

"Hill," her douchebag friend from earlier said as he walked back over to us with the bimbo from before still attached to him. "This asshole bothering you?" He pitched his thumb in my direction, and it took everything in me not to snap the damn thing in half.

She swiveled around on her chair, staring him down with a scowl. "The only asshole bothering me, Blondie, is you and Babbette here."

"Belinda," the woman said, groaning. "It's not that hard of a name."

Sage's gaze swung toward Belinda, growing darker. "Betty, I just want you to know, Blondie here —" she pointed to her buddy but didn't look at him "—has the syph."

Blondie's eyes widened immediately, his face

turning fifty shades of red. "Why you got to lie like that? Damn, you're so fuckin' mean sometimes."

"The syph?" Belinda asked, gaping up at Blondie, twisting her overly processed hair around her fingertip. "Is that some award or something?"

Hill rolled her eyes, waving them off. "You two are a perfect couple, and this man—" she pointed toward me, and I held my breath "—has come to my rescue when my friend couldn't be bothered because he's too busy chasing some easy pussy."

Belinda placed her hand on Blondie's chest when his shoulders bunched up like he was about to blow his lid. "Baby, come on. I know so many other things we could be doing right now than talkin' to this mean-spirited prude snob."

But Blondie didn't move. He peeled the woman's hand away from his chest, holding it in his palm. "What rescue? What happened, Hill?"

"Just go away, Blondie. I'm not in the mood for you," Sage told him, turning her body back around on the stool. "Leave me alone for a few days, and you may come out of this with your balls still intact."

"Whatever you say, G.I. Jane Junior," Blondie said, backing away from the bar. "I plan on keeping my balls because someday I want kids, and I know you have the ability to take that away from me without even blinking. You're a cold, cruel woman. Why don't you take your friend here and maybe get yourself a piece of ass too? Maybe you wouldn't be so goddamn uptight and mean all the time."

"I'm not uptight, and I get plenty of ass," she spat back, suddenly sobering when she must've realized what she'd just said—and very loudly too.

"You wouldn't know ass if it hit you in the face," he told her, lifting his glass of whatever he was drinking to his lips.

Belinda snorted at his side, patting his arm. "You tell her, handsome. She's probably a lesbian anyway. I mean, look at her," Belinda said, throwing her arm toward Sage. "She's a lesbian if I've ever seen one."

I braced myself, knowing one of two things was going to happen. Either Sage was going to ignore the woman's comments, or someone—particularly Belinda—was going to end up with a fist to the face and flat on her back.

As Sage started to turn around, Blondie backed up, taking Belinda with him, probably knowing what was about to go down just as much as I did. I wasn't even this woman's friend, but I knew—as would any other man listening in on the conversation.

"You know what?" Sage said, bringing her eyes level with mine for a moment before glancing over her shoulder. "Fuck you, Blondie and the Bimbo Belinda. I'm not a lesbian. Never been a lesbian. And never will be a lesbian. I'm all about the cock, baby. And I also know I have what it takes not only to catch a man's eye, but to have him begging at my feet instead of me begging at his like a dog in heat."

All I could do was blink and stare, replaying her saying, "I'm all about the cock, baby."

Her green eyes swung to me before her mouth came crashing down over mine and proved to me just how right she was.

CHAPTER 3
SAGE

I STAGGERED BACKWARD, breaking the connection as soon as Austin snaked his arm around my back.

Swaying and light-headed, I gripped the bar, trying to steady myself.

Holy shit.

I locked my knees, keeping myself upright as I dug my fingernails into the wood grain. "I'm..." I shook my head, not sure what to say.

Austin blinked, lips parted, staring at me like he was in a haze. "I... You..."

I glanced around, looking for Blondie and his bimbo to give me shit, but they were nowhere in sight.

How long had we kissed? It seemed like only a minute or two, but then again, time had seemed to pass at a different rate as soon as my lips touched his.

I used to laugh at people who said they felt

something special when they kissed someone for the first time. Childish, I'd tell myself. Nothing but a fairy tale they'd bought into and convinced themselves they'd found their Prince Charming.

Was that what I'd just felt? No. The man in front of me wasn't royalty, but the bastard could kiss.

I blinked back at him, words still stuck in my throat. It wasn't like I'd never kissed a stranger before, but I was never the aggressor. "I'm sorry," I told him, dropping my ass back onto the stool next to him. "I didn't mean to drag you into whatever that was." I tilted my head toward the crowd behind us where Blondie had just been.

"Darlin'—" Austin smirked, the haze from earlier seeming to wear off "—you can drag me to hell if you want, as long as you kiss me like that again."

My cheeks heated at the same time my mouth gaped open, but still, I didn't have a smart, snarky reply. I just kept blinking and staring at him like a mindless moron.

I covered my face with my hands, hiding my embarrassment at my actions and words. "I can't believe I just…" I whispered, wishing I could disappear.

Austin's palms landed on my arms, trying to pull my hands away from my face. "Relax, Sage."

I splayed my fingers, sneaking a peek at the handsome man sitting next to me, not looking the least bit affected by what had just happened. "I need a drink."

"Clive," Austin called out, angling his body to see around me. "Emergency situation over here."

I groaned, closing my fingers and dragging my hands down my face. "Jack straight."

"You heard the lady," Austin told Clive as soon as he appeared.

"Make it a double," I added, knowing one wouldn't be enough to help ease the absolute horror I felt over forcing myself on a stranger.

Clive threw me a grin as he reached under the bar, fishing out a clean glass. "Don't let this one get to you," he told me, lifting his chin toward Austin. "He's an asshole, but not the biggest one in the place."

"I'm an asshole?" Austin said, touching his chest. "This coming from a man who married two women without them knowing about each other."

My eyes widened. "Isn't that illegal?"

Clive's smile shifted. "Only if the marriages were legal, which neither was. Being married by a shaman on the beach without a marriage certificate is more of a commitment ceremony than a real marriage."

My gaze slid to Austin, who was laughing, before going back to Clive. "Then what happened?"

He slid the empty glass in front of me and grabbed the bottle of Jack. "With?"

"The women."

"I still got them." He winked at me, filling my glass to the top with Jack.

I reached for the glass, wanting and needing the liquor. "But…"

Austin placed his hand over mine, stopping me from taking the gulp I so badly needed. "Trust me. Don't ask."

Clive leaned over, resting his arm against the bar. "Anything else, sweetheart?"

I wrinkled my nose at the nickname and how easily the word rolled off his tongue. "No. No. I'm good."

"There's always room for one more," Clive added, laughing his ass off from the look of horror on my face.

"Fuck off, Clive," Austin told him. "She doesn't want to be your third."

Clive shrugged, throwing up his hands. "Never hurts to try. Never gain anything, especially a beautiful woman, without throwing the possibility into the universe."

I guzzled half the Jack in my glass, wondering exactly where my night had started to go wrong. I had an older man, close to my father's age, trying to make me part of his harem. My best friend ditched me for some woman who meant nothing to him and never would. And then there was Austin…a man I'd kissed and didn't even know.

When I joined the navy, I promised myself I'd

change my ways. I'd grow up. Become the adult my parents always wanted me to be. But within minutes of walking into the bar, I'd kissed a complete stranger.

"So, G.I. Jane Junior?" Austin raised an eyebrow. "Want to explain that to me?"

I waved him off, wiping my lips with the back of my hand. "It's nothing. Just Blondie being Blondie. Tell me something about you. Where are you from? Kentucky? I hear the slightest twang."

Austin sighed. "Twang?" He laughed. "You're definitely not a linguist, darlin'. I'm originally from Tennessee, but moved to Florida when I was seventeen. And then, after I joined the navy, I've been everywhere."

"Why Florida?" I asked on a whim, trying to keep him talking about himself and not asking about me.

"You want the long or short version?"

"Long."

Austin slumped a little, leaning over the drink he'd been nursing. "When I was seventeen, my mother was murdered."

I gasped, my hand flying to my mouth. "Oh my God. I'm so sorry."

He turned his head, giving me a sad smile. "Thanks. It feels like a lifetime ago, but every time I close my eyes, I see it."

"See it?" I asked, concerned and confused by the dark change to his demeanor. I felt guilty now for asking him about his past, wanting to keep the focus away from me. "We don't have to talk about this. We can talk about something else."

"It's fine. It doesn't hurt talking about it anymore."

I placed my hand on his arm, giving him a light squeeze. "I'm so sorry."

"Men were after my father and murdered my mother to get to him. After that, I was sent to live with my older brother in Florida, and the rest is history."

"Wait…" I placed the glass I was about to take a sip from on the bar, giving Austin my undivided attention. "You just said a whole lot in only a few words. I need a minute here to digest everything."

"I've had years, and I barely believe it either." He took a sip of his drink, staring behind the bar, his face unreadable.

"And your brother?" I asked, still reeling.

Austin turned to me, a small smile on his lips. "He's a good guy. Took me in after we hadn't seen each other for a decade. He put a roof over my head, fed me, and put up with my bullshit long enough for me to graduate and enlist. Do you have any siblings?"

I nodded, wondering if I would've been able to raise Sawyer if something happened to our parents. "A little brother. He's a complete pain in the ass."

"It's our job to be a pain in the ass."

An uneasy silence suddenly developed between us. I was rarely at a loss for words, but as I sat next to Austin and he told me some heavy things, I felt the weight of those words and his life experiences. "Blondie calls me G.I. Junior because my parents are kind of kick-ass."

Austin's blue eyes sparkled. "Kind of?"

I shrug. "I don't usually talk about them, but since you…" I let my voice drift off because I didn't want to recount what he'd just stated. I gazed down at my drink, hand gripping the glass tight. "My dad was a SEAL, and he's still totally badass." I chuckled, swinging my eyes to Austin. "But I'll never admit that to his face."

Austin laughed, lifting his drink to his lips as he turned his body toward me. "And your mom?"

I sighed. "She was FBI," I blurted just as Austin was swallowing a mouthful of Jack.

He choked, eyes watering as he struggled to get the whiskey down his throat and catch his breath. "FBI?" he asked between coughs.

I nodded. "I have some big shoes to fill."

"Wait, like, did she have a desk job at the FBI?"

I pursed my lips, rolling my eyes. "She did not push papers all day. She was an agent in the field."

"So." He coughed again, covering his mouth, and paused for a second. His eyes were glued to mine. "Your dad is a former navy SEAL, and your mom worked for the FBI. Are you shitting me right now?"

I waved my hand at him, rolling my eyes. "Well, no, I'm not shitting you."

He laughed, his perfect white teeth gleaming. "We could not have come from more different worlds."

"But here we are, same place, same time, same life." I smiled, liking the way he looked at me when I spoke.

"So, let's circle back to your comment outside."

I tilted my head, trying to remember everything that had happened and was said, but there had been so much even in the short amount of time. "What comment outside?"

"You could bust my arm without breaking a sweat." He didn't even blink when he repeated my ridiculousness back to me.

I chuckled. "Well…" I drew out, covering my mouth as I chewed. "I wasn't lying. My parents made sure I could take care of myself even if I didn't want to learn. I could probably teach you a few moves."

The smirk on his face was nothing short of glorious as he placed his hand on his chest, laughing. "You're going to teach me?"

I nodded, laughing too. "Just because you're a man doesn't mean you couldn't learn something new from a girl."

"You're going to teach me?" he repeated, tapping his chest with his palm as he blinked a few times.

"Uh, yeah." I smacked his shoulder playfully. "Since you bought me dinner, it's the least I can do."

He shook his head and bit his lip, stifling his laughter. "You're a piece of work."

I dipped my head. "Thank you."

"Nineteen-hundred hours at Pete's Gym."

I blinked. "What?"

"For my lesson." He grinned, running his hand up his shirt to his neck. "I want to make sure I'm able to defend myself in case someone attacks me," he teased. "And don't make me wait. If someone jumped me over the weekend and you didn't give me my lesson, you'd feel really guilty."

I balked. "I would not."

His beautiful grin spread into the most sinful smile. "Darlin', you would."

"Fine. Fine." I threw up my hands. "Pete's Gym."

The look of satisfaction and smugness he wore fit him well. He was yanking my chain, and I knew it. I'd learned enough from my parents to read someone, especially when they were trying to play me. Austin whatever-the-hell-his-last-name-was was definitely working me.

"Nineteen-hundred hours."

"I know."

"Promise me you'll be there?" he asked, running his hand over the back of his neck, kneading the muscles.

"I always follow through, Han Solo."

"I don't know enough about you to make that determination yet, Dynasty."

"Dynasty?" I asked, almost choking on a bite I'd just taken of the burger.

He leaned back, soaking me in, making me feel more exposed and bare than I would've felt being naked in front of him. He was studying me, forming an opinion about me without even knowing me. "Your mom is a secret agent, your dad is a 'badass'— your words, not mine. So, yeah. You're part of government royalty. You're part of the Dynasty."

"You're crazy."

"Crazy-hot, yeah?" He winked, the smirk rising on his lips.

And goddamn it if my cheeks didn't heat from that one simple move I'd seen come my way dozens of times in my lifetime. But for some reason, in this moment, with this guy who was, of course, hot too, my body decided to respond.

"You're pretty."

The single word was enough to make his cocky smirk falter. "Pretty?"

I nodded, giggling like an idiot. "So pretty with your blue eyes and long eyelashes."

"Been staring?" he teased, fluttering the lashes on the very eyes I'd been trying to avoid as much as possible.

Everyone had a weakness. A part of the human body that was their downfall. Mine was eyes. They were the windows to the soul. They had the ability to express so many emotions without much movement. Austin's eyes were nothing short of spectacular. The depth of the blue was only rivaled by the intensity of the pain, no doubt from his past, he'd tried to hide.

"No," I shot back, lying.

Based on the way his mouth curved, he knew I was lying too. "Whatever you need to tell yourself."

My phone vibrated next to my plate, pulling me away from the look of satisfaction on his face. "They're here," I said as soon as I saw the text from roadside assistance.

For the first time, I didn't want them to be early, but like all things, nothing was ever what we wanted, but what the world decided to give us.

"I've got to run." I climbed down from the stool, grabbing my phone to text back the person waiting outside. "Thanks for dinner."

"Tomorrow," he reminded me, not asking but telling me.

"Tomorrow," I replied, pitching my thumb over my shoulder as I backed away from him like if I didn't start moving, he'd capture me in his orbit, and I'd be unable to escape.

"Want me to come outside with you?"

I shook my head, placing my hands out in front of me. "No. No. I got this. Trust me."

He dipped his chin, giving me the out I so badly wanted and needed. "Give 'em hell, Dynasty."

God, he was gorgeous and older. Maybe a few years older than me, but he wore it well. Unless you were close enough, the fine lines around his eyes weren't noticeable. Maybe it was his past that left the markings on his face, making him appear older than he really was. Life could do that. Stress could be a bigger bitch than time.

The heat back in my cheeks, I turned, giving Austin my back and heading for the door like my ass was on fire. No man had ever left me feeling even a little off-kilter. No one before him, that was.

It was hard to explain something I'd never felt before. It was like he knew me, but he didn't. Like he had me all figured out, when he couldn't possibly after only one meal. But there was still something that had me running for the parking lot.

As I touched the door handle, I turned, giving him one last look.

"Fuck," I muttered, hating myself as soon as his eyes locked on me.

He winked and waved, making it very clear he'd caught me.

"Fuckin' fabulous."

Why did I do that?

I'd never been a look-back girl. Not under any circumstances and definitely not when it came to a man.

I was drawn to those pretty blue eyes, the cocky smirk, and arrogant attitude. He was the perfect combination to be my next great mistake.

It didn't take a genius to know I had a pattern and a type. Love them and leave them was my pattern, but

Austin didn't completely fit the mold of the previous guys I'd been with.

Sure, he was cocky and arrogant, a trait I'd found myself drawn to time and time again. But I usually stuck to the jocks, forgoing the military type because I wasn't looking for another father figure. I'd had enough bossing around my entire life. And I sure as hell wasn't about to sign up for a lifetime subscription.

CHAPTER 4
AUSTIN

LEANING OVER, I rested my elbows on my knees, trying to catch my breath.

"How long you going to stare at that clock?"

"Fuck off, old-timer," I grumbled.

Walter, a man I'd met a decade ago, who also owned the gym, laughed as he dead-lifted more weight than should be possible at his age. "She's got your balls all twisted. She must be something."

"She does not."

He grunted as the weights hit the floor. "Knew it."

"Knew what?" I growled, rubbing my forehead to stop myself from watching the seconds tick by.

"Only a sweet thang could have you acting a fool." He shook his head, letting out a louder laugh. "Known you since you barely had any short hairs, kid. Never known you to be a clock watcher. Put two and two together..."

"I just met the girl," I said defensively. Too defensively, actually.

"Ah," he crooned. "New love."

I hopped up, bending my neck side to side to keep loose. "Whoa. Whoa. Not new love, Walter. She's just some woman I met."

"Some woman?" Sage's voice carried over the classic rock as she stood behind me, no doubt with her hand on her hip, ready to throw down.

"Dynasty," I muttered. "You finally decided to show up?"

When I turned, she was standing exactly as I expected. Hand planted firmly on her hip, one shoulder cocked, and a perfect eyebrow raised. "Ready to get your ass kicked?"

"Yep. Put a fork in him. He's done," Walter whispered next to me, making damn sure I heard his words.

I stared at her, taking in her long legs covered in tight black spandex, showing every curve. The tank top she wore was formfitting with the words printed on it dipping in all the right spots. She was nothing short of delicious. "Darlin', I know you probably have a mean jab and can maybe knock me on my ass, but there's a big issue we have to discuss."

She lifted her shoulder higher, along with her chin, showing no fear and oozing attitude. "I will knock you on your ass, Han. So…" She shrugged as her eyes roamed down my body and back up to my face, taking their sweet-ass time. "I don't know what we have to discuss."

I cracked my knuckles and stepped closer to her. "If I lay a hand on you, my grandmother would haul ass down from Tennessee and whip my behind. It's going to be hard for me to defend myself without possibly hurting you in the process."

Sage stalked forward, chin high, defiance radiating off her. "Listen." She craned her neck, staring up at me with the most brilliant green eyes. "I laid down the challenge. I told you I'd put you on your ass. Now, if you don't want to stop me, that's fine. But I don't do weak, and right now, it sounds like you're being a pussy."

I jerked my head back at the insult, but goddamn if I didn't like hearing that dirty word falling from her lips. "I'm not being a pussy, darlin'. I'm being a gentleman."

"Pussy," Walter coughed, diverting Sage's attention away from me.

She smiled, throwing her hand his way. "Even the big guy agrees with me. You're making excuses. I don't need you to be a gentleman. I'm tougher than I look, and no matter how much bigger you are than me or how wide your biceps are..."

"You noticed my guns, huh?" I winked at her and flexed, sending her eyes rolling back.

"Kind of hard not to when they're the size of most men's thighs."

I kissed my left one, being a complete and total tool in the process, but I knew she was watching. Knew she was salivating to touch them too. "I work hard at these."

"You done with the self-love, Han Solo?"

Walter burst out laughing, and as soon as my eyes cut to him, he did an about-face and stalked off. But he didn't stop laughing, muttering under his breath about how I'd met the one girl who could handle my bullshit and who gave it back better than I dished it out.

"Why, Dynasty, you wanna help?" I teased, knowing I was crossing a line.

Her eyes narrowed as she shook her head. "There's something wrong with you."

"If there's something wrong with me, then I don't want to be right."

"For fuck's sake," she muttered, lifting her face toward the dingy ceiling of the gym. "Let's get this over with. I got shit to do and places to be."

"Don't be in too much of a hurry. I may not be able to fight back by hitting you, but I will do everything in my power to make it impossible for you to put me on my ass."

Her eyes sparkled as the smile returned to her face, and she dropped her bag in the middle of the floor. "I see we have the gym to ourselves. Didn't want an audience for your ass-beating?"

Her attitude totally gave me a boner. The girl was

not only beautiful, but the mouth on her sent shock waves through my system like no one else ever had.

She sauntered to the ring in the middle of the gym, lifting the ropes to climb inside. I stood there, frozen, unable to move as I gawked at her ass, and unable to stop myself from doing so. But just as she turned, I broke out of the haze, finding my voice and my sanity.

"I had some work to do today and couldn't be here any earlier. And for your information, I didn't want an audience because I figured no one needed to see you lose, not the other way around."

She motioned for me to follow, pointing to the floor in front of her. "Come on. It's time for me to spank your ass."

I rubbed the back of my neck, stalking toward the ring. "That shouldn't sound so sexy," I whispered.

"What?" she asked, staring at me.

"Nothing," I said quickly, climbing through the ropes to stand right where she had pointed. "How do you want to do this?"

The words were barely out of my mouth before she was coming at me. Right hand up, leg sweeping out, trying to take me down. But I moved too fast, making her catch nothing but air.

"You're a quick little thing," I teased as she bounced up and down like I'd seen professional fighters do. "Be careful, or you're going to wear yourself out."

She chuckled, paying my shit-talking no mind. "I could do this all day. I may be a girl and a sailor, but I have more tools in my arsenal than most."

"I have no doubt." I smirked, knowing she probably had more tools in her arsenal than just about everybody, except for a select few. No child of an FBI agent or former SEAL would grow up without learning more than the basic moves. "We'll see who's where when this is over."

"You're so damn chatty for a dude. You really are scared of me."

"I am not," I started to say, but she'd moved across the mat like something out of a video game, leg in the air again, swinging for my head. I ducked, saving myself a black eye. "Don't mess up my mug. It's my best asset."

"Debatable." She shrugged, finding her footing and acting like this was part of her everyday life.

I moved around, each of us stalking the other. "What's my best asset then, darlin'?"

"What's mine?" she threw back.

The answer was easy, but should I be honest? Fuck yeah, she was beautiful. Maybe the most beautiful creature I'd ever laid eyes on, but it wasn't what I liked best about her. "You've got a great ass." It wasn't a lie, but it wasn't the thing that made my heart skip just a little when I'd heard her voice earlier.

"Typical," she muttered.

"And mine?"

"I haven't found one yet," she said, laughter in her voice.

"Liar," I teased, flexing my arms again, watching as her gaze flickered to their movement.

"Shut up," she growled, lurching toward me, but I turned, thinking I was going to save myself from the brunt of her fists.

But I wasn't thinking, and I knew better than to leave a blind spot, showing my back to anyone, especially the enemy. In that moment, Sage was my enemy, and she took the opportunity to use my misstep against me.

She hopped on my back, wrapping her legs around my waist and locking her elbow around my neck. I gasped, twisting in a circle, and pulled at her arm. If she were a man, I'd drop back, crushing them under my weight.

"Say you give up," she whispered in my ear, the sound so sweet and opposite of what was happening.

"Never," I gasped, grinding my teeth together as I pawed at her arm.

"Do it, and this can all be over."

I tightened the muscles of my neck, knowing they were no match for the muscles in her arms. "Baby, why would I do that when your tits are pressed so tightly against my back?"

She growled, trying to tighten her hold but losing ground. "Fuckin' meathead with all these muscles," she said, releasing her grip, but not climbing off me.

I could feel the heat of her core against my lower back and the fullness of her breasts near my shoulders. Damn, the only thing better would be if we were naked and doing this.

"You know you love how hard I am."

She loosened her legs, sliding down my body, but before she retracted her hands from around me, her palm slid down my body, moving over the front of my sweatpants. She palmed my cock through the thick material, her mouth still near my ear. "Not too bad," she whispered.

I closed my eyes, sucking in a breath, holding myself back because I thought I'd crossed every goddamn line already, and she most definitely had now. "Dynasty, hands," I warned, knowing I only had so much strength when it came to a woman groping me.

Her hand disappeared, along with the heat of her body before there was a palm to the middle of my back, pushing me away.

"Give up?" I asked her, hoping she wasn't, because so far, this had been more fun than I'd had in a long time.

"Never." She pushed her hair back, breathing deeply like she was a little winded. "Do you?"

"I'll quit if you agree to go on a date with me."

She blinked, staring at me like she didn't believe the words coming out of my mouth. "What?"

"I'll concede this fight if you go on a date with

me," I repeated, wanting her to know I was dead serious.

She giggled. "If you want a date, you have to beat me. I don't date weak men."

I laughed, grabbing my stomach as I doubled over. "Weak?"

She nodded, tapping her foot, arms crossed over her chest. "So far, I haven't seen much strength, but if you want a date, you have to earn it, buddy."

I wouldn't allow this to be the end of whatever was between us. If I had to put her on her ass, I'd do it. But doing it without touching her with my hands would be tricky. Not impossible, but not easy either. "Bring it, Dynasty," I told her, motioning for her to come at me.

I only had one way to bring her down without laying my hands on her. As she lunged forward, coming at me like a curvy wall, I did the only thing I could do in a situation like this; I fell forward, taking her with me.

My hands hit the mat first, my hard body pressing against her softness next. Her eyes widened as my cock pushed against her leg. "Good enough?" I asked, smirking down, our mouths so close together I could feel her warm breath.

She pushed against my chest, wiggling underneath me. "This doesn't count."

"Does too," I argued, not letting her up from underneath me.

She felt good like this. We felt good like this. The fire in her eyes burned brighter. The fierceness and determination on her face only made her more beautiful and alluring. "You're flat on your back. You never said I had to use my hands."

She struggled a few seconds more before finally going limp underneath me. "I can't help that you're as big as a tank," she groaned. "That's not fair."

"We didn't make rules, baby. You just said you'd put me on my ass. But right now, it's your ass we're resting on."

She grunted, pursing those pretty, pouty lips. "You're a jerk."

"Never claimed I wasn't, but you still want to go out with me. I just gave you a reason to say yes without you having to admit you want me just as bad as I want you."

Our breathing was heavy and fast, matching each other breath-for-breath. We stayed like that, staring at each other, breathing erratically, neither of us speaking for longer than I'd ever thought possible. The air crackled around us, buzzing with energy and sexual attraction.

The moment her pupils dilated and her cheeks turned a deep shade of pink, there was no more denying what she felt. She couldn't. "Um." She licked her lips, sending my cock into a tizzy, and smirking when she felt the fucker move. "That's a negative. We can't…"

Eyes locked. Hearts pounding. I lowered my head, leaving almost no space between our lips. "We can't what, darlin'?"

She blinked slowly as her breathing grew more ragged and shallower. "We can't do this. I can't do this."

We were so close I could see the flecks of brown in her irises, swimming in the sea of green. "You can't date?"

"I made a vow," she whispered as her gaze moved to my lips. "I can't break it."

"A vow? Are you secretly a ninja navy nun?"

She slid her hands up my arms, resting against my biceps, squeezing just enough for me to know she was checking me out. "No, dumbass. I promised myself that I wouldn't have any one-night stands. And since you're just passing through"—she said those two words like they were acid on her tongue—"that makes whatever this is impossible."

I pulled back a little, staring down at her face, taking in the bow of her lips. "Aww, Dynasty, I'm flattered. But who said anything about having sex? I think I asked you for a date, which in my world, means dinner and talking."

She tightened her hold on my arms, digging her fingernails into my skin. "If you only wanted to talk, you wouldn't be on top of me right now."

I dropped my head back down, so our lips were almost touching again. "I haven't stopped thinking about your lips since last night," I admitted in a moment of weakness. "Dinner, talking, and a kiss is my reward for this."

She smiled up at me. "And based on what's pressing against my leg, you've already had your sweet reward, Han Solo."

"If that's the case, I'm not moving anytime soon," I told her, loosening my elbows enough to lower more body weight against her. "I'm really comfortable and enjoying myself."

She raised her head from the mat and narrowed those fiery eyes. "Old shoes are comfortable."

"Shh," I whispered, shaking my head slowly and closing my eyes. "You're ruining my moment."

"Arrogant," she grunted, wiggling again underneath me. "Self-absorbed, cocky motherfu—"

"They all mean the same thing, darlin'," I said softly, interrupting her, enjoying the fuck out of her softness and sass.

"You're still a…" she started to say as I opened my eyes.

Without thinking, I did the only thing I knew would make her quiet.

I kissed her.

CHAPTER 5
SAGE

I STARED at my reflection in the mirror, running my fingers across my lips, still able to feel the warmth of his mouth on mine. I groaned, hating the way I felt about a man I barely knew.

Was I in love? No. We'd only known each other a day, and I'd never believed in love at first sight.

But was I in lust? Hell yes, I was.

Austin was relentless, and no matter how many times I protested, he sucked me in, making me agree to another night out with him. He kept telling me his time was limited here, and once he left, I'd regret turning him down for the rest of my life. The man was so full of himself.

"I was really hoping you'd stay in tonight and help me organize," my roommate, Allison, said to me as I grabbed the tube of my favorite mascara.

"Tomorrow," I promised her, moving my face

closer to the mirror to apply the first layer to my eyelashes. "I can't cancel my plans, but I promise I'll make it up to you."

She crossed her arms, leaning against the doorway to the bathroom, staring at me. "You've been here less than forty-eight hours, and you've already found a man."

Allison, Blondie, and I had met at A school, where we'd learned the basic ins and outs of our jobs in the navy. I'd really wished I could room with Blondie, but instead, I was stuck with Allison. She was nice. Don't get me wrong. But her idea of fun and mine were two totally different things.

But after the shit Blondie pulled at the bar, he was on my shit list, at least for a little while.

I pumped the wand a few times, coating it with the thick, black mascara, staring at her in the mirror. "I wasn't looking for a man, Al. He's only in town for a few days, and I promised him I'd go to dinner with him before he leaves."

"So, I haven't lost you forever?"

I shook my head. "You could never lose me."

She rolled her eyes. "As soon as we get settled, you're going to find yourself a guy, one who's staying, and I'll never see you again."

I kept my eyes on the mirror, running the wand across the top eyelashes of my right eye. "You're being a tad bit dramatic."

She sighed. "Am not."

That was Allison. Overly dramatic about the dumbest things.

"As long as I'm stationed here, I'll be living with you. I'm not leaving to run off with some guy." I turned my head toward her as she shook her head. "Really, Al. Why don't you start on the kitchen, and tomorrow night, I'll help finish it?"

She chewed her lip, staring at me as neither of us moved. "I don't know. I can finish the kitchen by myself, but maybe tomorrow, we can organize the bathroom."

"Sounds fun," I muttered, not even trying to hide my lack of enthusiasm.

"So, who is he?" she asked as I turned back toward the mirror.

I opened my eyes as wide as possible, applying a coat of mascara to my left eye. "Don't know too much. He's navy, but only passing through. Here on official business."

"What's his rate and rank?"

I shrugged, careful not to blink and mess up my makeup. "I actually have no clue."

"Is he older or younger?"

"Older."

Her eyes widened, matching mine, but for very different reasons. "If he's higher rank than…"

"You've asked me more questions about him than I've asked him about himself. I know he's stationed in

California, but he grew up somewhere in Florida. That's about all I know."

"You can't date a man who's…"

"We're not dating," I told her, cutting her off from going down that road. "We made a bet. I lost, and I'm paying up."

"You're going out with him over a bet?"

I nod. "I always keep my word."

She pushed her jet-black curls over her shoulder and rubbed the back of her neck. "I know. That's why I know tomorrow's going to be so much fun."

"It is?" I asked, furrowing my brows. "Why?"

"We're going to organize the bathroom, silly." She smiled.

"How could I forget," I mumbled.

She clapped her hands together, humming to herself as she moved away from the bathroom door toward the kitchen.

Our apartment was small but more space than we'd have living on base in an old barrack. We each had our own bedrooms, shared a bathroom, and had a big enough living room for a television and the most comfortable sofa we could afford.

My phone vibrated on the counter, drawing my attention away from my makeup. "Hey, Dad," I said, my voice more chipper than usual.

"Someone's in a good mood," he replied. "Enjoying your new place?"

"It's so big, it's like a palace."

Dad laughed, knowing I was full of shit. "What's on tap tonight?"

"Just going to stay in and organize the kitchen with Allison."

"That's what you're doing on a Saturday night?"

"Well, being an adult isn't always fun and games, Dad."

"Now you're sounding like your mother."

"You're such a liar," Allison said as she walked past the bathroom with a box labeled "Pots and Pans" in her hands.

I shot her a warning glare, and she kept moving, laughing the entire way.

"Did you eat dinner yet?" he asked, clearly not hearing Allison.

"In a bit. Allison's whipping up something now." I lied to my dad again, something I rarely did and always felt guilty for afterward.

"Just wanted to make sure you were okay."

"You could've just texted me."

Dad grunted. "You know I'd rather hear your voice."

"Aww. You're missing me, big guy?"

"The house is too quiet without you here."

"Maybe Sawyer could use a phone call."

"Your mom's on with him now. We drew straws, and I got you."

"You got the better end of the deal, ya know."

"I do." He laughed. "Anyway, I'll let you go. I'm sure Allison could use your help."

Dad had loved Allison the one time he met her but could instantly tell she was a little uptight. To a parent, she was a dream roommate. She didn't like to party…ever. She was too disciplined and organized to let a night out with friends undo everything she worked so hard for.

"I'll text you tomorrow."

"Call me tomorrow."

I groaned. "Fine. Fine. I'll call you tomorrow if I have time because I have watch."

"Then you won't have time."

I snorted. "Dad, the navy is very different from when you were here. I'll have my phone with me."

"When I was in, we had to write letters or wait in line for the phone. You're all spoiled and don't know how good you have it."

I rolled my eyes. "Is this where you're going to tell me about having to walk a mile to school in the snow?" I teased him.

"Shut up, kid. Go help Allison and tell her hello."

"Bye, Dad," I said, drawing out his name.

"Later, sweetheart. Love you."

"Love you more." I smiled at the phone, staring at his photo on the screen as I tapped disconnect.

"Holy fuck!" Allison yelled from the living room.

I ran out of the bathroom, grabbing my pants off the counter and trying to put them on without falling on my face. They were halfway up my legs when I rounded the corner, finding Austin and Allison staring at each other. I backed up a few steps, peeking around the corner, spying on them.

"Um, hey," Austin said to Allison, giving her a small wave. "I'm Austin."

"Well, fuck me," she muttered, sounding more like me than her usual, more reserved self.

"Excuse me?" he asked, blinking, his forehead wrinkled and confusion all over his face.

"You're the bet. Holy shit. What are you?" she whispered, stepping back like she needed more space to take in every last inch of the man.

He tilted his head, gawking at her. "What am I?"

She nodded. "Yeah, man. You're not a normal-sized human being."

He almost choked. "I'm normal."

"You're big." She stretched her arms out as wide as she could. "Like, unreal big."

He smiled that crooked, sexy smile. "I know."

I yanked up my jeans, fastening the button and hiking up the zipper before I made myself known. "Hey," I said, slowly walking out of the hallway into the living room. "Ready?"

Allison turned to me, her eyes as big as saucers. "Holy fuck," she mouthed, waggling her eyebrows.

I winked at her, knowing she would want all the details now. I forgot we'd decided he'd pick me up at our place, doing the whole chivalry thing. He refused to let me meet him at the restaurant because that wouldn't be proper. "I'll be back in a few hours."

"She'll be late. Don't wait up," Austin added.

"Go have fun." Allison practically pushed me out the door when I got near her. "I want all the details," she whispered in my ear.

Austin smirked with his eyes trained on mine. "She'll have plenty to share."

I gazed across the water as the sun began to touch the horizon. The warmth of earlier had started to fade, but the small grains beneath me were more than enough to keep me from being cold. "This is so beautiful."

"There's nothing like a Florida sunset," Austin said, inching his body closer to mine. "I never really appreciated a sunset until I moved here."

"The sunrises in Virginia are something else."

His fingertip grazed mine, and I didn't move away. "Before the service, I don't think I was ever awake early enough to see the sun come up, and if I was, I didn't stop to look."

"I'm sure I'll see a lot of beautiful sunrises and sunsets when I deploy next month."

"Already headed out?"

I turned my head, staring at his face bathed in the

orange glow of the setting sun. "Already. It's going to be a long seven months."

"Deployment can suck, especially your first, but you'll hit some awesome places."

"I guess, but I've been damn near everywhere. My parents weren't ones to staycation."

Austin stretched out his legs, dropping back onto his elbows. "I hadn't been anywhere until I joined the navy. I went from bumfuck Tennessee to middle-of-nowhere Florida. I hadn't been outside the United States until I enlisted."

I spun my ass in the sand, turning to face him as I pulled my legs to my chest. "What's your rate?"

There was so much I still didn't know about Austin. While he was chatty, he was also standoffish. Maybe that was from his past. The tragedies he'd lived through made him keep things close to the vest. He only let me graze the surface of the real man underneath.

"Let's not talk about work anymore," he said, watching the waves rolling over the sand a few feet away. "It's nice to get away from it all and act like someone other than a sailor."

I pulled my legs tighter against me, resting my chin on my knees. "Sure," I told him and then fell silent.

I didn't know what else to talk about. We barely knew each other. Besides the navy, we didn't seem to have much in common.

"How old are you?" I blurted out, trying to fill the silence.

"Twenty-nine. You?"

He was older, but not as old as I'd thought. He was handsome but looked like he'd been through some shit in his life.

"Twenty-three."

"And it's your first deployment?"

"I went to college and finished my degree before I enlisted."

He raised his eyebrows, looking impressed. "Smart. OCS, then?"

"I thought you didn't want to talk about work." I didn't want to explain why I didn't join the ranks as a commissioned officer, opting to enlist like most everybody else I knew.

"Fine. You're right."

The silence returned, settling around us as I moved my gaze away from him to the same point on the horizon where he was staring.

"What are you doing next weekend?" he asked out of nowhere as he placed one hand over my bare feet.

I snapped my gaze back to his face and gaped at him. "Next weekend?"

"I have to take a run down the coast to see my brother and figured I could use a little company."

I blinked, still in shock. He wanted me to go home with him? We'd known each other for less than a day, and he wanted to take me home. He seemed to be working a little fast, especially since there was no future for us.

"Well…" I paused, trying to think of an excuse even though I didn't have to work. "I don't know. Why me, Austin? We don't know each other, and introducing me to your family is kind of a big deal."

"It's my last weekend in town, and I hate going down there alone. Everyone's so damn happy, and then there's me, the third wheel the entire time." He sat up then, placing his legs on either side of me. "I promise I'm not trying to trick you. I just need a partner in crime for the weekend. Someone who can help take some of the heat off me."

"Um…" I hesitated, buying myself time and trying to come up with a good excuse. I mean, it was weird he asked me to go home with him. Most of the men I'd dated, even for an extended period of time, never introduced me to their families. It wasn't something I was used to dealing with or even knew how to do.

"Never mind," he said, drawing his hand back from my skin.

"No. It's not that I don't want to, but…" I sighed. "Why me?"

"Why not you?" he asked, like I was insane for even questioning him. "I thought you could use a weekend away, have a little fun, maybe have some good, homemade food."

I raised an eyebrow. "Your brother's a chef?"

Austin laughed. "He's a shit cook."

"I'm confused. You just said good, homemade food, and since you only have a brother, who's going to make all the food?"

Austin sat up, facing me, curling his fingers around my ankles. "My brother's a tattoo artist, but his girl's family is the best family ever. After my brother took me in, they made sure I felt like I was one of them too. And the grandmother…" He hummed, closing his eyes. "She makes the best Italian food you'll ever taste."

I wasn't shy, and God knew I loved to eat. I hadn't had a decent home-cooked meal in so long. I'd been running on ramen and burgers for months, opting not to eat the navy food if I could. "How many people are we talking?"

Austin shrugged. "I don't know. There're maybe thirty of them."

My eyes widened. "That's a small army."

"I lied. There are more than forty if you count all the kids."

"Fuck," I muttered. "Forty people is a lot."

"You'll never have to see them again. Come on. Be my wingman. I want my brother to give me a tat while I'm there."

"Wingwoman," I corrected him, smiling. "And maybe…"

"What?"

"Maybe I want a tattoo too."

He smiled back, and in that moment, with the sun setting at our side, the sky a rainbow of colors, I knew I wanted to know more about the man sitting in front of me. I wasn't ready to say goodbye. I knew it would happen. Nothing permanent could be possible with us living on different coasts. We belonged to the government, and that trumped everything else.

But with the dimming sunlight shimmering off his eyes, I said, "What the hell. I'm game."

CHAPTER 6
AUSTIN

"SO, dipshit, where have you been the last few nights? I've called you a few times," my brother, Pike, asked as I walked across base, hustling my ass to get a cup of coffee.

"Around," I replied.

He grunted. "Already found a woman, didn't you?"

"Maybe," I drawled, hating that he knew me so well. "But she's different from the others. We're just friends."

I could hear his eyes rolling through the phone. "I've heard that before."

"No. No. I've never said that about anyone. Don't lie and put words in my mouth."

"You fall in love with every woman you sleep with."

I laughed. "I haven't slept with her. I told you, we're just friends, Pike."

He gasped. "Is your dick broken?"

"Ha-ha." I lifted my chin toward a fellow sailor as he passed by.

"She must be something special or ugly as sin if you haven't fucked her yet."

"I'm bringing her home this weekend as a friend."

There was silence for a moment.

"Is that okay?" I asked.

"Austin's bringing home a girl, darlin'. You okay with that?"

Gigi, Pike's better half, squealed in the background. "Give me the phone. I need details."

"Just put me on speaker so I don't have to repeat this shit over and over again."

"You're on speaker," Gigi said, her voice filled with excitement. "Tell me everything. Who is she? How long have you known her? What's she do?"

I rubbed my temple, already getting a headache, knowing exactly how the weekend was going to go before we even pulled in the driveway. "We just met a few days ago, and we're only friends, Gigi."

"And you're bringing her home?" Gigi asked.

"Well, I figured she could use a weekend away, and it's such a long-ass drive. Besides, I'm always a third wheel."

"You've never brought anyone home, though," she

reminded me. "And you're never a third wheel. You're family."

"I know. I know. Don't read too much into this. We're not getting married or anything."

"He hasn't slept with her," Pike told her as soon as I finished my sentence.

"This is a big deal," Gigi said, speaking quickly. "A huge freaking deal!"

"It's not a huge deal. She had the weekend off, and I had somewhere to be. I figured she could use a weekend away before she heads out on deployment."

"Mm-hm," Pike muttered. "A home-cooked meal."

"Shut up. You know there's nothing like Grandma Gallo's food."

"They'll be excited to see you. Everyone will be. It's been a long time since you've shown your ugly mug around here."

After my mother died and my father was put away in prison, Gigi's family embraced me during a time I'd felt completely lost. I was a complete douchebag too. I had a chip on my shoulder, dealing with so much baggage, guilt, and confusion, but they put up with my shit. Not only put up with my anger but made me feel like I was part of the family from the very first time I met them.

"I can't wait to see everyone. I've missed them," I told them, feeling the warmth in my chest I rarely let myself experience. "I can't wait to be back, even if it's only for a weekend."

"Why don't you leave the military when your contract is up?" Pike asked.

"Leave and do what?"

"I'm sure you could work with James and Thomas at ALFA."

That was always Pike's fallback plan for me. He wanted me to join their security firm and settle down nearby, but I wasn't ready. I had a life to live, a world to explore, and nothing was going to stop me from following that dream until I was too old to perform my duty.

"Someday, brother. Someday."

"What time will you be here on Friday?" Gigi asked, ignoring our conversation. "And will she need her own bedroom?"

"Yes, to the two bedrooms, and probably around dinnertime."

"I'll cook something fabulous," Gigi replied.

"It's going to be an interesting weekend," Pike said. "I'll let Tamara, Mammoth, Lily, and Jett know you'll be in too. I'm sure they'll want to see you before Sunday dinner."

"Whatever you want to do. It'll be nice to be home for a few days and relax."

I'd never thought Florida would feel like home, but after all these years, especially after being away, it did. I'd fought the feeling for a long time, but then I realized it was about the people around me. My brother, his girl, her family. They all welcomed me, making me feel like I'd always been part of the family.

"Ditto," Pike muttered.

"We want to get some tats on Saturday. Can you schedule us in? Probably two hours max each."

"You got it. Gigi and I will make time for you two."

"I got to run, guys. Work's about to start," I lied, done with all the mushy stuff. "I'll text you when we're heading down."

"Take Route 19 and not I-75," Gigi told me.

"I'm not new, babe," I said because she'd told me that more than once over the years. "We will."

"I'm so crazy excited to have my little brother home," Gigi said, making me feel all warm and fuzzy.

I'd never had a sister. Never thought I wanted one. But after being with the Gallos, I realized you could never have too much family, and sisters weren't as bad as guys made them seem.

"Love you, guys. Talk soon."

"Love you too," Pike said.

"Love ya bunches," Gigi added before the call disconnected.

I hurried to the building, craving coffee no matter how shitty it was going to be. Caffeine was caffeine, and right then, I needed a shit-ton.

"Look who decided to show his pretty face today," Maverick, a SEAL I'd known for four years, said as he kicked back in the chair with his arm slung over the back of the next. "Long night?"

I gave him the middle finger before taking a seat across from him. "I see you're still your same asshole self."

He shrugged before he pushed a cup of coffee toward me. "Life's never been better. Sun's shining, I'm sitting on my ass, sipping a coffee. No bullets coming my way today—or, at least, not yet—but I'm ready to get this shit finished and my ass back to California ASAP."

"Where is everyone?" We'd planned to meet and have coffee before we headed into our briefing about today's activities, but so far, I hadn't seen another soul I knew.

All I saw was a bunch of kids, looking way younger and greener than I thought I had when I'd first enlisted. As I looked around the room, I felt like I was sitting in a private high school cafeteria and not the mess hall on base.

"Partied too hard like you, my friend," Maverick said, lifting his cup toward me with a slight tip. "I turned in early, opting for a good night's sleep over someone's sloppy seconds."

"Your entire life has been sloppy seconds," I told him, laughing. "Stop acting like you're all about the classy pussy. You're the biggest slut I know, Mav."

Maverick ran the palm of his hand across his freshly shaven jaw, hiding his smile. "Speaking of pussy, are you heading home this weekend to get a piece of ass? Maybe see an old flame, flash your medals and uniform, and have a girl on her knees in under a minute?"

"You're really an asshole."

His smile grew. "It takes one to know one."

"Aren't you two cute," Wiz said, standing at the end of our table with Trigger as they stared at us.

"Fuck off," Maverick replied, not even looking in their direction. "Get your coffee and sit your asses down. We have shit to talk about before we go into today's bullshit."

A second later, Wiz and Trigger were gone, heading toward the line of young sailors waiting for their morning grub.

"What's going on?" I raised an eyebrow, not used to seeing Maverick so serious about anything except a mission. "You seem off today."

"Lyndsey wants me to join the civilian ranks."

I blinked, staring at him like he had two heads. "You going to listen?"

Maverick and Lyndsey had been dating on and off for years, but never did I think they were serious enough for her to tell him how to live his life.

He rubbed the back of his neck, gazing to the right as he adjusted himself in the chair. "I don't know, man. Sometimes I know how lucky I've been to have lived through some of the shit we've been through, and I feel like I'm ready for a desk job."

I blinked again, wondering who'd been scrambling his brain. "Listen, if you want out, get out. But for fuck's sake, don't do it for a woman."

"You hate Lyndsey, don't you?"

"No. Of course not," I lied. The woman was a bitch, always trying to lead him around by his dick. "She's great."

He gave me the side-eye. "I can tell when you're full of shit, and you're full of shit."

"What did we miss, ladies?" Trigger asked, sitting down next to me as Wiz sat down next to Maverick.

I threw my hand out toward my friend. "Maverick wants out."

Trigger and Wiz sat there, stunned and silent.

"Lyndsey wants him to sit behind a desk," I added.

"Ain't no pussy worth that," Trigger said, shaking his head. "Not after all the shit we went through. She's either with you or against you, and right now..."

Maverick put up his hand. "I know. I know." He sighed. "Don't say it."

"Wiz, how's your marriage going?" I asked, knowing full well the torment he'd been going through for the last year.

He lifted his coffee to his lips, staring at me across the table over the rim. "Shit couldn't be better," he grumbled, not selling his line of bullshit to anyone at the table.

I laughed first, followed by the other two.

"She's spending the money faster than I can make it. At this rate, I'm going to have to leave the service, become a contractor, and sell my soul back to the navy to keep up with her purse and shoe addiction."

"I'm fucking staying single forever," Trigger stated, lifting his chin. "Never getting my balls held hostage by a chick. Too much pussy without all the complications out there to let myself be tied down or twisted up by only one."

I rolled my eyes. "I don't see any women falling at your feet, begging for your dick, Trig."

"Didn't know you were so interested in my cock, man," he said, but my gaze drifted across the room, finding Sage walking through the crowd.

I placed my hand next to my face, hiding slightly, trying not to be too overt. Sage looked stunning in her uniform, with her hair tied back, twisted in a bun. Her neck was long and regal, cheekbones even more pronounced without her hair framing her face.

"What are you doing?" Mav asked, eyebrows furrowed as he stared at me.

"Nothing." I turned my body, facing Wiz. "We ready to get out of here? We have ten minutes to hustle across base, or else we'll get our asses chewed out."

Maverick looked around, not moving to stand. "Who's here?"

"No one," I bit out, climbing to my feet. "We got shit to do and places to be."

"Austin?" Sage's voice came from behind me.

My gaze flickered to Maverick first and his shit-eating grin as he turned his face up toward Sage. As he opened his mouth, I spoke up, stopping him in his tracks from saying something shitty and embarrassing.

"Hey, Hill." I turned, putting a smile on my face. "It's nice to see you, but we were just heading out."

"Oh." The smile on her face fell. "Just wanted to say hi. I didn't mean to interrupt or overstep."

Trigger coughed. "Awkward," he muttered.

"You're not overstepping or interrupting," Maverick said, sliding out of his chair to look down on the beautiful brown-haired woman. "I'm Maverick, Austin's best friend." My real name coming out of his mouth sounded foreign.

Sage held out her hand to Maverick, smiling. "I'm Sage."

"Austin, you didn't tell us about your new friend," Trigger added, eyeing me and the lack of rank clearly displayed on her uniform.

"We just met the other night, and we're only friends, dickhead."

Thankfully, we weren't in uniform, and the obvious misstep on my part wasn't as clear to her. She was lower rank, something that could get me in major trouble. There were rules in the military for everything, including relationships.

"Just friends," she repeated, smile unwavering. "I've got to run. I have duty and am just grabbing a cup of coffee to go." She pulled her hand back from Maverick's and lifted her gaze to me. "It was good to see you."

"You too, Sage." I smiled, somehow keeping my shit together, but knowing I was completely awkward and stupid as fuck.

I stood there, watching as she walked through the crowd. She didn't look back or sneak a peek over her shoulder as she moved farther away from us.

"So, already found yourself some fresh pussy," Wiz said, elbowing me in the ribs.

I shook my head, rubbing my neck. "Her car battery died, and I waited with her. Nothing happened. Like I said, we're only friends."

"That right there," Trigger said, ticking his chin toward her swaying hips and fine ass, "is nothing but a heap of trouble."

"We're friends," I repeated, sounding less convincing every time the words came out of my mouth.

Wiz hooked his arm around my shoulder, trying to put me in a headlock. "Whatever you say, Casanova." He laughed, dragging me toward the door and away from the one person who could quickly and easily kill my career.

CHAPTER 7
SAGE

"HOTTIE ASK YOU OUT AGAIN?" Allison asked, bumping me with her hip as I jumped the line to stand by her side.

"No."

"Well, why the hell not?" She craned her neck, trying to see him as he disappeared. "You should've asked him out, then. I mean, he was hot as fu—"

"Allison," I chided her, looking around as the people near us started to stare.

She moved closer as we shuffled forward. "Come on. He's totally into you."

"Did he look like he was into me?"

She shrugged one shoulder. "Maybe not with his buddies around him, but he's totally into you." She waved her hand in between us. "I mean, look at you. Even in uniform, you're a sex kitten."

I rolled my eyes. "I'm hardly sex kitten material."

"Whatever."

I grabbed a paper coffee cup, dumping cream and sugar inside before filling it with coffee. "He can probably have anyone he wanted."

"You're talking like you couldn't do the same. There isn't a guy in this room who wouldn't lick your boots clean."

I giggled, picturing a man with his tongue dragging across my boot, worshiping me. "You're ridiculous."

"I am not. What do you want to do this weekend?"

I grimaced. "I'm busy this weekend."

She snapped her head around toward me. "Doing what?"

"Nothing important." I started to walk away, but Allison rushed to my side. "I have to go out of town for a few days, so you'll have the apartment to yourself to scratch whatever itch you have going on down there."

She raised an eyebrow, studying my face. "Out of town where?"

"Down south."

"We are south."

"We're in Northern Florida. There's much more to this state."

She grabbed my wrist and stopped me from walking farther. "You're going with him, aren't you?"

I gazed over her shoulder, staring off in the direction he'd disappeared. "I'm not."

She gasped, gripping my wrist tighter. "You're a liar. You were going to run away with him and not tell me."

"We're not running away," I whispered, looking her straight in the eye. "His brother works in a tattoo shop, and we're going down there to get tattoos."

She gave me a crooked smile. "There're tattoo shops here. It doesn't require a trip."

"But his brother isn't here. I swear, nothing is going on between us."

She dropped her hand and stepped back, watching me closely. "Did he kiss you?"

"No," I answered too quickly.

Her eyes widened. "Friends don't kiss."

I winced, trying to downplay the importance of the kiss and the playfulness of the moment. "It was like kissing my brother."

"Mmm-hmm." She smirked. "Keep lying to yourself."

I lifted my chin and started walking, heading toward the ship and out of the mess hall. "Let's go, MacGyver. We have duty."

Austin: Meet me for a drink tonight.

Me: I don't think it's a good idea.

Austin: Y?

Me: We could get in trouble.

Austin: For having a drink?

Me: Austin...

Austin: Live a little. Trust me.

Later that night, I leaned against the side of my Jeep, grinning at my phone as I reread the text messages, waiting for Austin to arrive.

Why was I there? I had no idea. I always thought I had a good head on my shoulders, but there was something about him that had my brain not working right. Maybe it was his haunting blue eyes or his cocky smirk that drove me mad.

"Lookin' good, darlin'." His sweet, barely there, Southern drawl crawled across my skin, warming me.

I pushed off the Jeep, turning toward the sound of his voice. I drank him in, soaking up his handsomeness with the setting sun as the backdrop. "You're not so bad yourself."

His smile morphed, turning sinful. "If you weren't looking at me like that—" he tipped his chin toward me "—I'd almost believe you didn't find me extremely attractive."

I chuckled. "Extremely?" I waved my hand at him, dismissing his arrogance. "You're so full of yourself."

He laughed as he reached into the bed of his pickup truck and grabbed a six-pack of beer.

"I thought..." I tilted my head, confused as I gawked at his arm muscles.

"You were worried about an audience, so I figured we could sit on the beach and share a drink in private."

"You know I hate sand between my toes. I told you that the last time you made me go on the beach," I reminded him. It was something people always found odd about me. I hated how the tiny grains felt and how they clung to my body like a second skin.

"You seemed to enjoy it the night we met," he said with a shitty smirk that made my toes curl.

I glared at him, lost for words.

"This is better than the bar, though. Quieter too. I got us covered," he said, reaching into the back with his other hand, pulling out a blanket.

"Well, didn't you think of everything." I smiled, unable to say no to this man. "You're pretty slick."

"Not slick." He winked. "Prepared." Austin ticked his chin toward the beach at the edge of the parking lot.

I took a step, staying back for him to walk at my side. "Sorry about this morning. I shouldn't—"

"Don't," he said quickly. "I was an asshole."

"I still should've minded my place."

He stopped walking and grabbed my hand. "Your place?"

"Yeah. You know..." I shrugged and frowned.

"We're friends, Dynasty. There're no rules about

friendship. I freaked out when I shouldn't have." His finger ran across the underside of my wrist. "I'm sorry."

"Don't apologize. We weren't entirely honest with each other about some things like rank. No matter if we're friends or not, rank matters in the military, and so does perception."

"Let's sit and talk. I only have a few more days here before I have to head back to California, and I don't want to spend the time apologizing to each other about bullshit."

A weird wave of sadness came over me. "I don't want to either."

His hand didn't leave mine as he started walking again. This didn't feel like a friendship. I never held hands with Blondie. Never. But I wasn't about to pull away.

As soon as my sandals hit the sand, my feet sank and the tiny granules slid between my toes. "How far are we walking?" I asked, sounding whiny and like a complete girl.

"Just a little farther." Austin pointed toward the wet sand around twenty feet ahead. "I like listening to the waves. It's calming, and I always sleep better."

"Whatever you want."

He gazed at me, one eyebrow up. "Whatever?"

I smacked his arm, laughing. "Come on, Han Solo. There's a beer with my name on it, and I'm thirsty."

I followed him down the barely illuminated beach to where the waves rolled up on the sand, waiting for him to lay out the blanket. He was quick, spreading out the soft gray material and motioning for me to sit first. I dropped down, careful not to put my sandy feet on the blanket to contaminate our spot.

When he sat, he didn't leave much space between us, grabbing two beers from the six-pack and twisting off the tops. "Fair winds and following seas," he said, clinking the glass bottle against mine before I had a chance to lift it to my lips.

"What's deployment going to be like?" I asked before taking a sip of the cool liquid.

"It'll suck for the first few months before you settle in and realize there's no turning back."

"Fantastic," I muttered against the rim.

"It's not that bad. You get to see some pretty cool places even though you're not there for long."

"When was your last deployment?"

He didn't say anything for a minute, just stared at me. "It's been about five years since I've been deployed on a ship for any extended period of time."

I almost choked. "Five years? How is that even possible?"

He stared straight ahead, not giving me his eyes. "I haven't told you everything."

"I figured that much," I muttered.

Austin leaned back on his elbows, stretching out his legs. "I'm a SEAL," he admitted softly.

"A SEAL?" I asked, knowing the answer before he confirmed my suspicions.

"Yeah."

"It's honorable and dangerous."

"Honorable?" He laughed. "Maybe. Dangerous… sometimes. I just wanted to do more than I was after I enlisted. I love what I do now and can't imagine doing anything else in the world."

I peered over my shoulder at him. "No SEAL imagines doing anything else with their lives until it happens."

"I felt the need to do some good after my father did so much bad."

I kicked off my sandals, brushing the sand from my feet before I turned on the blanket to face him. "What did he do exactly? You don't have to tell me, though. I know we just met, and it's none of my business."

"It's not like it's classified information. He was greedy and got involved with the wrong people. The men he worked for were looking for something my father stole and tried to use us to draw him out by killing my mother."

"I'm sorry."

He shook his head. "I'm only sorry my mother was sacrificed for his greed. My father can rot in prison forever. You're lucky, though, Sage. You have good parents."

"I know," I replied, resting my arms around my

knees. "I never knew how lucky I was until I was older."

"What was it like growing up in your house?" he asked, twisting the beer bottle in his palm. "I've been around loving families who were selfless and caring, something I didn't experience much of as a kid."

"I don't think I could've had a better childhood. I wasn't the easiest kid. I was a little too wild for them sometimes, but they loved me just the same."

"My dad used to be that way, but he changed over time. After a while, my brother disappeared because he couldn't take all the hate in our house. He moved in with my grandma, and when he was old enough, he took off for Florida and I didn't see him for almost ten years."

I couldn't imagine not having Sawyer around growing up. As much as he drove me crazy, he was all that I had besides my mom and dad. He knew everything about me, and I knew all there was to know about him too.

"That had to be hard."

"It was, but the only blessing after my mom died was getting my brother back in my life."

"Tell me about him."

Austin laughed quietly. "He's an interesting character."

I stretched, putting my feet out and resting them near his upper body. "How so?"

"He lived with a biker club for a while."

My eyes widened. "He did? He was in an MC?"

He shook his head. "No, he just crashed at their compound."

I furrowed my brows. "How does one crash at a biker compound?"

"He got shot, and they took him in like a wounded puppy. He lived there for a few years, learned tattooing, and once he was on his feet, he left."

"They let him leave just like that?" My mouth hung open, shocked.

"He wasn't a member of the club. He's still friends with the guys and everything. He sees them from time to time. But he moved near Tampa to take a job at the most well-known tattoo shop in the area and is with the owner's daughter."

"Oh, that has to be interesting."

"I worked there for two summers with them, and they're perfect for each other. The family, her family, took me in and made me feel like I'd always been there."

"They sound like something special."

"They are." He smiled as his eyes flickered from me to the rolling waves. "They're the best type of people."

"Are you sure you want me to come with you this weekend? Won't it be weird? We don't even know each other."

"Do you trust me?" he asked, his eyes coming

back to my face and studying me. "I promise it'll be a great time."

"I don't know." I sighed. "Won't people think we're…"

"They won't think anything. You'll be saving me from a weekend of being the center of attention."

"You want me to take some of the heat."

He nodded, smirking. "It's easier to share the Gallo attention than to be the only one standing in the spotlight."

"You promise you don't have an ulterior motive?"

He tipped his head back toward the sky. "What other motive could I have?"

I shrugged. "I don't know. Maybe you're trying to lure me away to have your way with me."

"Darlin'," he drawled, bending his neck so his piercing eyes were on me. "If I wanted to have my way with you, I wouldn't have to take you five hours away."

My stomach fluttered at his words. "Not true, cocky jerk."

His smirk grew. "You don't have to come. I'm sure you'll find something more interesting to do this weekend. I don't need a chaperone or a babysitter."

"I really wanted that tat, though," I said softly, sounding so weak and like I was making an excuse. "And you said he's the best, so…"

"He is, and so is Gigi. She's amazing. If you want the best tattoo possible, Inked is the place to get it."

"Well, I certainly don't want a shitty one."

"What do you want to get?"

I gazed down at the blanket, embarrassed. "I don't want to tell you. You're going to laugh."

He lifted his hand, dragging his fingers over his heart. "I swear I won't laugh."

"No. You'll have to wait and see. I'm not letting you kill my dreams ahead of time."

"I'm not a dream-killer, sweetheart. I'd never laugh at you about anything."

"Liar," I told him, raising my eyes to look at him.

He lifted up on his palms, bringing his body so close to mine, I could feel the warmth from his skin. "You know what I want?"

I gulped, blinking slowly, unable to drag my gaze away. "What?" I whispered.

He sat up, pulling off his shirt, giving me a full view of so many muscles, my mouth instantly watered. I wouldn't stare. I wouldn't stare. I kept repeating those words in my head as I stared.

"A swim." He raised an eyebrow, cocky sinful smirk firmly planted on his face. "You game?"

"It's dark."

"And?" He stood, unfastening the button on his jeans.

I couldn't tear my eyes away from his body, flicking my gaze to his crotch one too many times. When I finally looked at his face, he was watching me, smiling, knowing I was looking way too hard. "Have you ever seen *Jaws*?"

"Are you scared, little girl?" he teased.

I growled and jumped to my feet, yanking off my tank top, revealing my sports bra. "I'm not scared of a little water. I'm more worried about a handsy SEAL."

He lifted his hands in the air, stopping from unzipping his pants. "I'll be nothing but a perfect gentleman."

I shimmied out of my shorts, pushing them down my legs before kicking them to the side.

"Nice panties." He smiled, his eyes roaming my body.

"Shut up. They're comfortable. What about you? You a tighty-whitey guy?" I laughed, covering my mouth with my hand while I stood there practically naked.

He barked out a laugh. "Don't be ridiculous." A second later, his pants were gone. He stood there with his long, muscular body and only a pair of skintight black boxers.

Even in the dim lighting from the parking lot, I could make out the outline of his cock. I had to run. I couldn't stand there, staring, wanting, gawking. "First one to the water is a rotten egg!" I yelled as I took off toward the waves.

God, I was an idiot. But a second later, he was on my heels, chasing me into the warmth.

It didn't matter how fast I moved. He moved

faster. I made it a few steps into the water when his hands grabbed my waist, hauling me backward like I weighed nothing at all.

I squealed and kicked the air as my body came out of the water until my back collided with his chest.

"Where you going, little girl?" he whispered in my ear in such a deep tone, my skin pebbled.

"Austin," I said into the darkness, feeling my cheeks heat even though the rest of me shivered.

"You can't get away that easy." His lips brushed my ear, sending another round of spasms, but this time, they were between my legs.

I turned my head until our lips were almost touching. "You're too fast."

"When I want something bad enough, I'll move heaven and earth to get to it."

I swallowed, searching his blue eyes lit only by the moonlight as the air crackled and the waves splashed around us. "I…" The words died in my throat as he turned me around in his arms, while my feet never touched the sandy bottom of the Gulf. "Hey," I breathed as we came face-to-face.

His eyes studied me, and I felt the weight of that stare and felt connected to him. More connected than I'd felt with almost anyone before.

The waves crashed into us, but Austin held me tight, standing like an unmovable rock in the water. The stars shimmered overhead like a million pinpricks of light shining only for us.

No other words were spoken before he leaned forward, taking my mouth with his. The sounds of our labored breathing filled the space between us as we clung to each other.

He kissed me hard and deep, with one hand tangled in my hair, holding me still.

This was how a kiss was supposed to feel.

My skin tingled, my lips stung, and every bit of me wanted every bit of him.

Fuck. I was too far gone now, and that wasn't a good thing either.

CHAPTER 8
AUSTIN

I LAY IN THE SAND, gasping after my morning run. I'd pushed myself too hard, needing to get some of the frustration out of my system from last night.

I wanted Sage so badly, but I needed to be careful not to cross any more lines. I promised her we were only friends, knowing we had limited time before we parted ways.

Even if I were stationed here, we wouldn't work.

We couldn't, due to our difference in rank—not without being in a heap of trouble.

"Fuck!" I shouted into the damp morning air as the rays of the sun filled the sky overhead. I closed my eyes, resting my hands on my stomach as my breathing began to stabilize.

I should've left well enough alone. I shouldn't have seen her again after the first night. I knew better than that, but I never did anything the easy way.

My phone rang, drawing me out of my thoughts. "Hey," I said, answering my brother's early morning call. "Isn't it early for you?"

"Can't sleep."

I rolled forward into a sitting position and faced the waves. "What's wrong?"

Pike sighed. "I've been up half the night thinking about Mom. This is always a day when I have so many emotions."

It had been over a decade since she'd died, and yet, somehow it still felt like yesterday. I'd never forget finding her lifeless body covered in blood and the helplessness of being unable to save her.

"There's nothing you could've done to repair the relationship you two had. She made her choices, not you. She should've fought for you, but she didn't."

"I just wish I'd known how she felt before she died."

"At least she left you a letter and you knew afterward," I told him, curling forward to rest my upper body on my knees. "We can't change the past, brother, and can only do the best with what we have for the future."

"I could never turn my back on my kid. What kind of person does that?" he asked me, his voice laced with pain.

"I don't know, Pike. Your version of Mom and mine were very different. I know you won't make the same mistakes as Mom did. That's her legacy, I suppose. None of us is perfect, she and Dad least of all, but just know we're not perfect either. We all have layers. Some good. Some bad. Don't live with regret, Pike. It's useless and destructive."

"When did you get so wise?" he asked.

"I'm hardly smart. I never seem to learn from my mistakes."

"What did you do?"

I collapsed back onto the warm sand. "I have my head all twisted about this girl."

"The girl you're just friends with?" He threw those words back in my face, knowing damn well I'd been full of shit when I'd called him the other day.

"It's complicated."

He laughed. "Women always are."

"This isn't just the typical complications."

"Do you like her?"

"Yes."

"Then what's so fuckin' complicated?"

"The navy, man. There are rules about dating outside your rank. Then there's the problem of being over a thousand miles apart."

"Whoa. You've really put some thought into this."

"There's something about her that I can't get out of my mind. I'm so fucked."

Pike laughed at my pain, always enjoying seeing me getting twisted over a girl. "Shit has a way of working itself out. Maybe after a weekend here, you won't feel the same way about her. You've only spent a few hours with her, and maybe after a little more, she won't seem so amazing."

"When did you know?"

"Know?" he replied, playing stupid, forcing me to say the words.

"When did you know you only wanted Gigi?"

Pike let out an even louder sigh than before. "When I met her in Daytona, I figured it was what it was. Just a fling. I thought about her after, wondered where she was and what she was doing. But when I finally saw her again, I knew I wasn't going to let her get away a second time. You that into this girl?"

I rubbed my forehead, squinting into the sunlight. "I don't know what I am anymore."

"You'll figure it out. You always do. And if you two are meant to be, you'll find your way back to each other. I never thought I'd see Gigi again, but fate brought us back together."

"When did you turn so damn sappy?" I asked.

"It's the Gallos, man. They rub off on you after a while."

From his lips to God's ears. The family had a way of changing a person. They could take the most hardened and jaded human and turn them into a pile of love and sunshine. They did it to Pike, and after a while, they sucked me in too.

"I better go. I have some shit to do before Gigi wakes up," he said. "I need to get my head right so I don't ruin our day."

"Pike?"

"Yeah?"

"I love you, brother. Whatever happened in the past is in the past. Leave it there. Don't let Dad's hate and Mom's mistakes ruin your future too."

"Never, Austin. Never. Love you too. See you this weekend."

"See you then," I said before disconnecting the call.

I watched the clouds pass overhead, shifting and merging in the morning sun. I'd been so busy with Sage, I'd almost forgotten the anniversary of my mother's death, something I never thought would happen. I still had nightmares about finding her. They came less often now than they did when I was younger, but that night still haunted me.

"Hey, stranger," a sweet voice said from a short distance away. "What are you doing out here? A little early to sunbathe."

I rolled onto my side, taking in Sage's long, tanned legs. "I could ask you the same thing."

Her skin glistened in the light, covered in the finest layer of sweat. "I just finished a run."

"On the beach?" I raised an eyebrow, knowing how much she hated sand.

Sage lifted a shoulder with a small smile. "It's a better workout than cement." Her smile fell as she studied my face. "What's wrong?"

"Nothing," I lied, not wanting to burden her. "Just tired."

"You're a shit liar, Austin." She dropped down onto the sand, crossing her legs. "Lucky for you, I have time this morning."

I sat up, brushing the sand from my hands. "Lucky for me, how?"

"I have time to listen while you talk. I don't have to be at the ship for a few hours."

"Darlin', while the offer is sweet, I don't have that much to say."

She tipped her head back and laughed. "Your mouth is always moving."

"Who taught you to ride a bike?" I asked her.

She furrowed her brows, blinking. "What?"

"Who taught you to ride a bike?" I repeated.

"My dad, of course."

"Not me." I shook my head. "My dad was never around."

"So, who taught you?"

"The maid," I told her, embarrassed and saddened by the reality that was my childhood.

Nothing about my life was typical. People looked at me as lucky since I'd grown up in a large house surrounded by material goods and servants. But nothing about my life was as grand as it seemed on the surface.

"Fancy and sad."

"I know, but that was my life. Anyway…" I

needed to change the subject. "I just got off the phone with my brother, and he's happy we're coming for the weekend."

"I could use a few days away from here," she said, drawing in the sand with her fingertip. "Besides Disney and the base, I haven't seen much of Florida."

"There's not much to see unless you're into trees and small towns."

She peered up from the sand, the sun hitting her eyes. "It's Florida. There has to be more here to see."

"The only difference between where my brother lives and Tennessee is mountains and hills. Florida's flat and boring."

"Well, I'm coming for a home-cooked meal. The scenery doesn't interest me as much."

I placed my hand over my heart. "You've wounded me. I thought you were coming to spend time with me."

She rolled her eyes. "Of course." She smiled. "You, food, and a tattoo."

"In that order?" I asked, studying her face.

"Sure. Whatever makes you happy."

I jumped to my feet, brushing the sand off my legs. "You're full of shit, Dynasty. Completely full of shit."

She placed her hand over her forehead, gazing up at me. "Where ya going?"

"Walking you home." I held out my hand, wanting to help her up. "You have duty, and I have a meeting. And don't forget to pack. We're leaving at first light."

She groaned, placing her palm in my hand. "Don't you ever sleep in?"

"I used to, but it's been years."

"You should work on that. Sleep's good for your body and your soul."

"Okay, Mom. I'll get more rest."

"Still lying," she teased, slipping her hand out of mine as soon as she found her footing. "But get some tonight, or else I'll drive, and you really don't want that."

"Why?"

"Let's just say I'm a bit reckless."

I gasped, not completely surprised by the revelation.

"My dad may have taught me how to ride a bike, but my mom taught me how to drive a car. I make the movie *The Italian Job* seem like child's play."

I nodded. "Good to know."

We walked across the sand to the pavement, only stopping to clean as much of the fine grains from our sticky skin as we could. When I was finished, I caught Sage staring at me.

"What?" I asked, still bent over.

"I wish you'd tell me what's wrong. You're off today. We may have only known each other a few days, but…"

"It's just a bad day, darlin'. I have them

sometimes. Seen bad shit. Done bad shit. It sticks with you after a while. It comes and goes, but by tomorrow, I'll be back to my old self."

"I miss the cocky asshole I met the first night."

"Oh, he's still here, and he'll be back tomorrow."

"Good." She smiled, eyes searching my face. "Head back to your hotel. There's no need to walk me back to my apartment. It's too far and in the opposite direction."

"I could use a walk to clear my head." I paused, biting my lip for a second. "Unless you're looking to get rid of me. Do you have a hot date waiting for you in bed still?"

She smacked my arm playfully. "No hot date unless you count Allison."

My eyes widened. "She's in your bed?"

She gave me a dirty look. "Don't be a dumbass."

"Comes naturally." I smirked.

We walked side by side, barely speaking, but a natural silence existed between us. There was no awkwardness like I'd felt with other people when I was too inside my head to chitchat. Sage let me have my quiet time without the pressure to talk.

When we arrived at her apartment, her door was ajar. "Wait," I said, grabbing her arm as she moved toward the door, ready to go inside. "The door's open."

"It's probably Allison. She's a little out of it sometimes."

"No," I whispered, gripping her a little tighter as I moved her behind me. "Let me check it out. I'm not letting you go in there first."

Sage peered down at where I was holding on to her wrist. "Listen, it's nothing. And if it isn't, I can handle whoever is inside."

I held up my hand and silenced her.

"Men," she muttered, motioning toward her apartment with her free hand. "Knock yourself out."

"Stay here," I told her, lifting her off to the side so she'd be out of the way in case someone ran out.

"Ridiculous." She rolled her eyes.

"Zip it, woman," I told her, hating that I had to argue with her about her own personal safety. I didn't care if she was G.I. Jane Junior or not, I wasn't letting her put herself in harm's way. "Do not move."

"What if there's gunfire? Should I run or just stay here and get shot?"

I pinned her with a glare.

She threw up her hands. "Fine. Fine."

I pushed open the door, looking around the apartment, and saw a man in the kitchen, opening a cupboard. I moved as quietly as possible around the space, staying low to avoid drawing his attention. He closed the cupboard door and opened another, searching for something.

His back was to me as I came up behind him, jumping on his back with my arm wrapped around his neck in a choke hold. He fought me, struggling as we fell backward, his full body weight landing on me.

I squeezed harder as he struggled for air, elbowing me in the ribs with all his might.

"Oh my God, stop!" Sage screamed as we fought on the floor. "Dad. Fuck. Dad."

I froze, releasing my grip. "Dad?" I gasped for air, my ribs aching and my chest tight from his weight.

As soon as I let go, the man, her father, elbowed me one more time, but harder than before, winding me even more. "Fucker," he grumbled, holding his neck with one hand.

"Daddy, Jesus. I'm so sorry," she said, bending down to help him off the floor.

He took her hand and climbed to his feet, glaring at me as I lay on the floor feeling like an idiot and a fool. "Who the hell is this?"

"Um." She peered down at me, her cheeks turning pink. "He's my friend."

Her father raised an eyebrow, still rubbing his neck where my arm had been. "Does your friend have a name?"

"Austin, sir," I said, finally climbing to my feet. "I'm so sorry. I didn't mean—"

He held out a hand, silencing me.

"He thought you were an intruder, Dad. You never said anything about coming here, and it's eight in the morning. What the hell were you thinking?"

He tilted his head, staring at her. "Allison let me in

before she left. I guess she didn't close the door. I wanted to surprise my little girl."

"Well, you did that." She laughed as she wrapped her arms around his waist, hugging him tightly. "I've missed you."

I stood there, watching them, knowing I should back out of the apartment quietly, just like I'd entered.

As I started to move, he slid his eyes to me. "Stop."

I didn't move another muscle. "Not moving, sir."

"Thank you," he said, catching me off guard. "Thank you for making sure Sage was safe, even if it cost me a few moments of..."

"No problem," I said, not even blinking. "She tried to come in here herself, but..."

"I can handle myself, and I wouldn't have attacked my own father, so..."

I rubbed the back of my neck, wanting to get lost. "I'm going to be late. I have to go, Sage."

She smiled. "Thanks for walking me home."

"You're welcome," I said to her before turning my gaze to her father. "Again, I'm sorry."

He gave me a chin lift as I backed away toward the door, getting myself away from the entire clusterfuck I'd just created all in the name of keeping Sage safe.

CHAPTER 9
SAGE

"WHO IS HE?" Dad asked as soon as Austin left.

"Just a friend I met."

"You've been here under a week, and you already have a friend who's willing to risk his life for you?"

"Well, kind of. Yeah." I raised my shoulder, wishing I could run to my room and away from the conversation. "He was just being a gentleman."

Dad's eyes didn't leave my face. "What's his full name?"

"Austin Moore," I said, wincing immediately, knowing I shouldn't have opened my big, fat mouth.

Dad took out his phone, pressed a button, and kept staring at me.

"What's up, man? Aren't you supposed to be visiting the kid and not busting our balls at work?"

"I want all the details on an Austin Moore. He's enlisted in the navy where Sage is stationed."

"Um," I muttered, inching backward. "He's stationed in California."

My dad's jaw ticked. "Scratch that. He's out in California. I want it within the hour."

"You got it. I'm on it," the man on the phone said before hanging up.

"You don't need to check him out. I can tell you whatever you want to know. He's only here a few more days." I collapsed back onto the couch, kicking out my legs and resting my tennis shoes on the coffee table. "You don't need to run an entire background check."

"I do. The man has been to your place, had his hands around my neck, and didn't seem right."

I sighed, rubbing my hand across my face. "Didn't seem right?"

"There's something shifty about the way he was acting."

"Shifty?" I laughed. "What does that even mean, Dad?"

"He couldn't have left fast enough."

"We're only friends," I groaned, pushing my head back into the couch cushion. "I swear. In a few days, he'll be gone, and I'll never see him again."

"Uh-huh," Dad muttered as he sat down next to me. "It's my duty as your father—"

"No," I told him, cutting him off. "It's not your duty to run background checks on every person in my life. You didn't do that with Allison."

Dad's gaze moved toward the floor.

I gasped. "You didn't, Dad. Please tell me you didn't have Allison checked out?"

"Well, I…"

"What is wrong with you?"

He placed his hand on mine, still shifting his eyes away from my face. "I'm a father, Sage. Your father."

"You know you're a weirdo, right? I mean, normal parents don't do things like this."

"If they could, they would," he argued.

I rolled my eyes. "I have to get ready for work. How long are you here?"

"Just until tomorrow. I'm here for work but wanted to spend some time with my girl." He smiled, reaching for my hand and giving it a light squeeze. "Can you make some time for your old man?"

I turned, curling into him, missing him more than I could even explain. "I'll always make time for you. Always."

"Good." He hugged me back, running his hand up and down my back. "I'm going to come to work with you and check out the ship."

I froze. "Dad…"

"What? I may have pulled a few strings…"

I sighed, knowing it was pointless to argue. Dad did what he wanted. He always had, and even as he aged, he never would or could change. "Fine. Fine. It's going to be boring."

"It's been forever since I've been on a ship. I wanted to see how things have changed."

All I could do was shake my head. "I'll be ready in five."

"That's my girl," he said as I pushed myself off the couch, walking toward my bedroom like I was headed to prison.

Today was not bring your dad to work day, but in Alex Hill's world, there were no boundaries, especially when it came to me.

I turned halfway to my bedroom, staring at my dad. "Did you call Chief and get the okay?"

He nodded, smiling as he kicked back, relaxing like he'd been in my apartment a hundred times.

"Do his background too?"

Dad's smile widened.

I huffed and stalked away.

Fathers were impossible, but mine really took the cake.

With my dad in town, I barely had time to do anything and that included talking to Austin about what happened. The day and night passed in a blur and Austin was quiet, hopefully busy with his training instead of ignoring me.

Austin: I'm so, so, so sorry, Sage.

Me: For what?

Austin: Choking your dad.

Me: Don't apologize. He kind of deserved it.

Austin: Kind of?

Me: He wasn't where he was supposed to be.

Austin: Which was where?

Me: At home in Virginia.

Austin: Plans dead this weekend?

Me: No. He's leaving in a few hours.

Dad peered over my shoulder. "Invite him to breakfast."

I craned my neck back, peering up at my dad as I turned my phone screen away from his prying eyes. "What?"

"Invite him to breakfast," he repeated, his face expressionless.

I blinked, confused. "Why?"

"Because a background check only tells me so much, and since my daughter is seeing this man, I want to know him better."

"Dad," I warned, tightening my grip on my phone.

He shot me a glare, the same one he used to give me as a little girl when I'd give him sass. "I'll invite him, but you need to behave."

"Don't I always?"

I snorted. My dad behaved as well as I did, which wasn't at all. "You better be nice."

"I'll be Mister frickin' Rogers."

"Who?" I furrowed my brows.

He pushed his fingers into his eyes. "I've failed as a father."

"You're crazy," I muttered.

"I'm going to call your mom and check in."

"She and I are going to have a long talk about you."

He laughed as he walked toward the patio. "And this is new how?"

Me: My dad wants you to meet us for breakfast.

Austin: Why?!?!

Me: He's insane, and he knows I'm going to see you this weekend. He wants to make sure you're not a serial killer. Don't mention where we're going this weekend.

Austin: So, you want me to lie to him?

Me: Yes!

My phone rang instantly. "Are you freaking insane?" Austin said as soon as I answered. "Lying to your father is like signing my own death warrant."

I laughed, glancing toward the patio to make sure Dad wasn't eavesdropping. "He'll never know. When did you turn into such a pussy?"

"A pussy?" he grumbled. "I know he's already checked into me."

"You do?" I chewed on the inside of my lip, wondering how I was the lucky one to be surrounded by so many crazy-ass men.

"Uh, yeah. You start asking questions about a SEAL, and word gets around."

"Oh. I'm so sorry, Austin. So sorry he's a bit…"

"He's a dad, Sage. He loves you. I get it. But asking me to lie to your father is inviting trouble."

"Pussy," I coughed.

The sliding glass door opened, and my dad poked his head inside the apartment. "He comin'?"

"Yeah," I told him, shooing him with my hand to go back outside. "He's coming."

"Good." He smiled, closing the door again, giving me some privacy.

"I won't tell him, but if he asks me flat out, I won't lie. I've never been a liar, and I'm not going to start now."

"For me, please," I begged, not wanting to have to go into a whole song and dance about being only friends and going home with Austin for the weekend.

"I'll think about it," Austin told me. "When and where?"

"Huffy's in an hour."

"I'll be there."

"Don't get there too early. Don't seem too eager," I told him, staring up at the ceiling and wondering how I could control the situation.

"What other rules do you have, Queen Bee?"

I laughed. "Shut up. Just be there."

"Roger that," he said before he was gone.

I waved at my dad when he peered through the glass, watching me. "Men are impossible," I muttered to myself.

An hour later, we were at Huffy's, my dad sitting next to me, placing me between the wall and himself. Austin sat across from us, looking relaxed and a little too hot with his wide shoulders and blue eyes.

"So, Austin, tell me about yourself," Dad said as he picked up the menu, eyes on Austin.

"What do you want to know, sir?"

"Whatever you want to tell."

"What didn't my background check tell you?" Austin asked point-blank, and I almost choked on my own spit.

"Man, the pancakes sound amazing, don't they?" I said, trying to break up whatever pissing match was about to go down.

My dad leaned back, laughing. "Word travels fast."

Austin raised an eyebrow as he stretched an arm out across the back of the booth. "You know how it is when you're a SEAL, sir."

"You've led an interesting life."

Austin nodded. "Wasn't one I would've chosen, but I've made the best of it."

"Done more than that, son. Most people in your circumstances would've gone another way."

Son? I turned toward my father, gawking at him. What in the world was happening?

"I wasn't going to walk down the same path as my father. Luckily, my grandmother and brother made sure my life didn't go to shit. We all have choices, and

I made the one that was best for me and my country."

Daddy sat quietly, staring at Austin, holding his menu for a moment. "It's honorable."

Austin shrugged. "College didn't feel right when I graduated high school. I couldn't very well sit on my ass and do nothing. The navy felt right, and once I was in, there was nothing I wanted more than to be a SEAL. Go big, or go home."

"How did you meet Sage?" Dad asked, changing gears as he often did with my friends. First, he made them comfortable, and then he started the real interrogation.

Austin's blue eyes slid to me. "Her Jeep broke down. I waited with her to make sure she was okay until they were able to get it fixed."

"I was more than capable of taking care of myself," I muttered.

"Maybe other places, but I wasn't going to leave you at the Rusty Knuckle alone."

Dad turned his head, glaring at me. "The Rusty Knuckle?"

I gave him an innocent smile. "It's just a little hole-in-the-wall bar. No big deal."

"I know what it is, Sage. I've been there."

"How?" I asked, tilting my head. "Is there anywhere you haven't been? I mean, honestly, Dad, you're so—"

"I've been to this base more than once. That place

has been around forever too. The one thing I do know is that it's not a place for a girl to be alone. Wait." He paused, his eyes narrowing. "Why were you alone? Wasn't Blondie or Allison with you?"

I toyed with the napkin underneath my fingertips. "Blondie was there, but he was busy with something."

Dad raised his eyebrow. "Busy?"

I nodded but then shook my head because I wasn't about to tell my dad Blondie was too busy trying to get laid to help me out.

"I should pay that kid a visit."

"Dad." I stared at him. "Stop."

Austin chuckled, and I shot him a warning glare.

"Blondie can't be with me all the time. Anyway," I sighed, glancing down at the menu instead of glaring at the two men sitting with me, "I could've handled everything on my own. I didn't need a babysitter, even though Austin took it upon himself not to leave my side."

Dad tapped the table with his finger, slowly and steadily. "I taught you how to take care of yourself, but that doesn't mean you won't need help from time to time."

"For the record," Austin added, "I wasn't babysitting you."

I peered up. "You weren't?"

He shook his head. "I thought you were…"

"A pain in the ass?" Dad said, laughing at his hilariousness.

"Ha-ha."

Austin chuckled and quickly covered his mouth when I gave him my full attention. "You were ballsy. You didn't need my help, but I still wanted to be there. You were all piss and vinegar."

"It's a trait she picked up from us. It's genetic, I'm afraid."

"Thankfully, I didn't pick up any genetic traits from my parents besides my looks."

"Well, that's a shame. They didn't do you any favors," I said, smirking at my funny, but just getting a straight face in return.

My father cleared his throat, drawing my attention. "Friends," he muttered softly under his breath. "This is how this shit starts."

"What can I get you?" the sweet little waitress asked as she walked over to our table, her eyes roaming the two men sitting with me. "Coffee, handsome?" She smiled at my dad, and I felt a little vomit rise in the back of my throat.

"Black, please." Dad smiled.

"And you, baby?" she asked Austin.

"Same, ma'am."

She blushed when he gazed up at her. I saw the change right before my eyes. "And you, darlin'?"

"Orange juice, please."

"Do you want to order now?"

I shook my head. "We need a few minutes, sugar," I said, throwing all the Southern flirtation back at her.

"Right on, sweet thing." She smiled, tapping her pencil against the little pad she was holding in her hand. "I'll be back in a jiffy with your drinks."

"You heading back to California today?" Dad asked Austin.

"No, sir. I'm going to visit my family for the weekend and then head back. Training's over, but I never miss a chance to see them when I can. It's been a while since I've had leave, with everything that's been going on in the world."

Dad nodded like he knew exactly what Austin meant. They'd lived similar lives, although in different decades. Nothing much changed in the military, and if it did, it took forever to happen.

"Family is the most important thing of all," Dad told him.

"Couldn't agree more."

"You only have a brother left?" Dad continued the interrogation, going over the details he'd been able to memorize from the short time he'd had Austin's file.

"No, sir." Austin rubbed the back of his neck, shifting in the seat. "I mean, I do, but I have more. My brother's wife's family is large, and they're mine too. They made sure of that."

"Family is more than blood," Dad replied.

I squirmed in my seat, not sure how I felt about my dad and Austin being pals, shooting the shit like they'd known each other for a long time, minus the questioning. "So, Dad," I said, pausing, waiting for their attention, or at least my father's. "Why the trip?"

"I'm heading over to Jacksonville for the day and then home tomorrow. I figured I was close enough to warrant a drop-in to see my only daughter."

"Two coffees and an OJ," the waitress said, interrupting all the awkwardness. "Ready to order?"

"Pancakes with bacon," I said quickly, ready to eat and run because this was all too much.

I wasn't in high school. Austin wasn't my boyfriend, but that didn't stop my father from questioning him like he was.

If Austin spoke to me again after breakfast, it would be a miracle. He'd probably tell me he'd changed his mind and would be heading to Tampa alone. I wouldn't blame him either if he did.

A few hours later, Dad wrapped his arms around me as we stood in the parking lot. "You stay safe. Don't get yourself into any trouble you can't undo or I can't fix."

Those words were code for don't get pregnant or run away and get married. "Daddy, come on. You've taught me better than that." I smiled up at him, staring into his green eyes, which were the same shade as mine. "I'm a good girl."

He brushed his lips against my forehead, smelling me like I was a newborn baby. "I know, sweetheart. I just hate having you so far away."

"I'm sure you're keeping tabs on me, even from Virginia."

"There isn't anywhere in the world you could go that I wouldn't."

"You're a complete weirdo." I laughed, placing my hand on his chest. "And a little much."

"I'm a worried father, looking out for his little girl."

"I'm not so little, Dad."

"I wish you were. I'd give anything to go back to the days of you running on the beach with the wild hair and cute laugh."

I curled back into him. "I love you, Dad."

"Love you too, baby," he said, and I held back the tears I knew would fall if I looked up at him again.

I didn't know when I'd see him again. I still had months before I'd have enough time saved up to make a trip back to Virginia worth the travel.

This was our goodbye.

CHAPTER 10
AUSTIN

"MAYBE I SHOULDN'T HAVE COME," Sage said, sitting next to me in the pickup truck. She fidgeted with the edge of her sundress, staring down at her knees. "You should be spending this weekend with your family."

"Don't be silly. It's just my brother and his wife tonight. They're cool people and completely no pressure."

Her attention shifted to me as I glanced at her. "Are you sure?" she asked.

"One hundred percent. Tonight, we'll have dinner and maybe go for a beer. Tomorrow, we'll get tattoos and then hit the beach if you want. Sunday, we'll eat with the family and then head back. It'll be no big deal."

"No big deal," she whispered to herself.

"They live at the end of this road." I ticked my

head toward the street, tapping my finger against the steering wheel as I tried to contain my excitement.

"When was the last time you were here?"

"It's been over a year."

"A year?"

"Time got away from me, and anytime I thought about taking leave, a mission would change my plans."

The normally sleepy street, empty of people with very few houses, seemed different from before. My stomach knotted the closer we got to their house and the cars lining the street stretched on for what seemed like miles.

"This is one busy street," she said, voicing exactly what I'd been thinking.

"Yeah," I said, laughing nervously. "Maybe someone's having a party."

The "someone" in this equation was my brother and Gigi or, more specifically, the Gallos. I should've known better. They did nothing small or quaint. There were no secrets either. I'm sure word had spread like wildfire as soon as I'd called my brother about my upcoming visit and plans were set into motion before we hung up.

Sage's gaze wandered down the line of cars stacked one after another on the roadside. "A very big party."

"Shit," I muttered as we pulled into the driveway, finding so many people gathered in the front yard, it looked like a block party. "I'm so sorry."

"Well," Sage laughed, "so much for a simple night."

"At least I can promise they're good people." My eyes wandered over the crowd as they turned toward the truck one by one.

"Only good people would do this." She motioned toward the crowd with an uneasy smile. "I hope they don't think…"

"They won't," I told her, knowing where she was going with the sentence. "They know me too well."

Her forehead furrowed as soon as the words were out of my mouth. "Gotcha."

"No. No. That's not what I meant."

"Doesn't matter. We're only friends, right?" she said, but there was something in her voice that caught me off guard.

"We are," I told her, shifting the truck into park. "Ready?"

She nodded, reaching for the handle. "Don't disappear on me. I'm not a shy person, but don't throw me to the wolves."

I chuckled. "They're not wolves. The only thing they will do is try to feed you. Don't resist. Just give in, or they'll hound you."

She smiled at me, her face lighting up brighter than the sun. "I could eat."

"I'll remember you said that," I told her as I opened the door and stuck a leg out.

Pike was the first one at the truck. My brother hadn't changed since the last time I saw him. Still a mess of wild hair, a scraggly beard, and big, blue-green eyes. Gigi was right behind him, pushing him out of the way to get to me.

"Austin," she said, jumping into my arms as soon as I had two feet on the ground. "Oh my God, I've missed you so damn much." Gigi squeezed me tightly, pushing the air from my lungs.

"Come on, darlin'. Let the man breathe," Pike told her, trying to pull her from my body. "Don't smother him."

She shot him a warning glare over her shoulder. "You better remove your hands if you want to keep them."

He threw his arms in the air, removing them from her. Pike tilted his head, rubbing his neck. "She's a bit cranky today."

"I'm not cranky, Austin. I'm excited to have my little brother home after all this time," she told me before she squeezed me again, burying her face in my neck.

I laughed, wrapping both arms around her back. "Missed you too, kid."

She arched her upper body back, gawking at me. "Kid? You've got to be shitting me. I'm older, fool."

I winked at my sister-in-law. "You don't look it."

She rolled her eyes as she finally released me. "Well, you haven't lost your touch, at least."

Pike didn't miss the chance to move her away, taking up the space in front of me. "I've missed you, brother," he said, stoic at first before he took me by the shoulder and pulled me into a giant bear hug. "You may be bigger than me now, but you're still a little asshole."

"Aww. I missed your sweet-talking," I told him, holding on to him like I'd done years ago when we were finally reunited after our mother's death.

He pulled back and grabbed my shoulder, eyes studying me. "You really look good. I'm so damn proud of you."

"Don't tear up on me, old man."

"Old man?" he grumbled, punching me in the arm. "She gets the compliments while all I get is lip."

"Just like old times." I smirked.

"Well, aren't you a vision," Gigi said, moving away from us and toward Sage, who had walked around the back of the truck, heading our way.

"Hi," Sage said, waving at us as her footsteps slowed.

"I'm Gigi, and this is Pike." Gigi pointed to my brother as he stood in front of me, before waving her hand toward the family. "And this is our family."

Sage tucked a lock of brown hair behind her ear, probably too petrified by the number of people gawking at her as if she were a zoo animal. "I'm Sage."

"Move it," Tamara said, pushing my brother to the side and grabbing me. "Damn, man. You're looking…"

"Hot?" I asked, cocking one eyebrow. "Or maybe sexier than ever."

"Hey now," Mammoth, Tamara's old man, said as he came up next to her, grabbing her by the waist.

"I was going to say you're looking old." Tamara laughed when I narrowed my eyes. "What do you think, baby?" she asked Mammoth.

"He looks like the same dipshit he did before, princess." Mammoth smirked, always yanking my chain and trying to piss me off.

A decade of my life, I'd been surrounded by these people. I'd barely had a relationship with my brother before our mother died and our father went to prison. He'd taken off when I was little, heading south, and left me behind. I couldn't blame him. Our parents treated him like shit. I would've done the same if I'd been in his shoes.

But their passing led me to Florida and a family that had taken me in and made me feel more welcome than anyone had before. Gigi, Tamara, and Lily were all close to my age, and I had been drawn to them to maintain any sense of normalcy. I'd had crushes on each of them at different times, but I was always more like their little brother in their eyes.

"Still a massive dickhead," I told Mammoth, holding out my hand to shake his. He wasn't touchy-feely like the other people in the family, but he wasn't as cold as he had been when he'd first brought his ugly mug around.

Mammoth smirked as he slid his palm against mine. "A man can't change his colors or ways."

"Ain't that shit the truth," I said, shaking his hand before I pulled him forward and wrapped an arm around his back.

He didn't even struggle. He gave in, giving me a quick pat on the back. "We're glad you are home for the weekend, kid. Even me," he whispered before clearing his throat and stepping out of my grip. "Ma'am. I'm Mammoth." He tipped his chin toward Sage as his wide frame shadowed her in darkness.

"So fitting," she whispered under her breath. "Hi, Mammoth." She gulped. No explanation was needed on his nickname. The guy was massive, covered head to toe in tattoos, and scary as hell. He was also sweet as pie and protective to those he loved.

I laughed, ticking my head toward the waiting group of family members near the front of the house. "You okay?" I asked her, reaching for her hand. "I know it's a lot to take in."

"No. It's great. Really great. You're so loved." She smiled, squeezing my fingers.

"I may have had some bad shit happen in my life,

but I am a lucky son of a bitch to have found this family."

I didn't even think I was within arm's reach when Suzy stuck out her hand and hauled me against her body. "Our boy is home and safe. Thank heavens. I've been so worried about you." She squeezed me until I couldn't breathe, but I couldn't wipe the smile off my face. "I wonder every day if you're okay. If you're eating. If you're sleeping."

"I'm doing all of that," I said, laughing as I hugged her back when she finally loosened her grip. "I'm great, Suzy. Couldn't be better, actually."

"You're so grown up." She smiled as she backed away, gazing at me. "So, so grown up." She repeated the words every time she saw me as if she'd imagined somehow time would stand still when I was away from them.

"Son," Joe said, coming to stand next to his wife. "We've missed you around here, and it's good to have you home for a few days."

"Joe," I whispered, tearing up a little. The man had been a father figure for me since the day I'd stepped foot in their lives. I'd been a complete shithead at first, but he'd taught me how to be a man and to be selfless and giving. "You have a few more gray hairs than last time I saw you."

He narrowed his eyes, pretending he was going to give me a right hook, before he threw his arm over my shoulder. "Life's been dull without you around."

"I know that's a lie," I told him, letting him pull me toward the door by the neck as my hand slipped away from Sage's. "There's no such thing as a dull day around here."

"Maybe when you retire from the navy, you can come back to work at the shop."

"I love you, Joe, but I don't think that's ever going to happen. I'll come back home when I'm done with the service, but I wasn't cut out to be a receptionist at a tattoo shop my entire life."

He laughed, nodding. "Well, I'll have to settle for seeing you every weekend."

"So, Sage, how did you meet our boy?" Aunt Izzy, Joe's sister, asked Sage behind me.

"My car broke down."

"Oh. Interesting. That's how Joe and Suzy met. Her car decided to take a shit, and my brother rescued her."

"Really?" Sage asked her. "You're not shitting me."

"I'm not shitting you," Izzy replied.

"Women," Joe muttered, rolling his eyes as he peered down and finally released me.

"Austin," Lily squealed, rushing toward me like hell on wheels. "God, you're a sight for sore eyes."

I smiled and instantly opened my arms, waiting for the girl I'd had the craziest crush on when I was younger. We never would've worked and never had a chance to get going, but the feelings had been there.

In a way, I still loved her, but I wasn't in love with her. She would always be my family, as was every person near me now.

"You're looking good, Lil," I said, feeling her round belly press into mine. "I see you've been busy again."

Jett, her husband, threw an arm around her shoulder and pulled her gingerly away from me. "I can't keep my hands off her."

I wanted to gag. Don't get me wrong, I liked the guy, but I'd always thought of Lily as mine. For that fact alone, no matter how great he was or how much she loved him, I still wasn't all about Team Jett.

"Sage, this is Lily and Jett. Guys, this is Sage."

"Hi," Sage said, sliding her hand back into mine, maybe feeling something in the air…mostly from Jett.

"Come. I want you to meet my husband," Izzy said, coming back up and looping her arm through Sage's. "And the rest of the family, of course. Plus, I'm sure you could use a glass of wine right about now."

"I could use something after that drive."

"Austin's been known to get a couple speeding tickets." Izzy laughed, pulling Sage away from me.

"I'm surprised he still has a license," she said.

"My husband and his other uncles have connections, or else he wouldn't."

"I have my own connections now!" I yelled out, glancing over my shoulder as Sage wandered away with Izzy.

Even though I had been looking forward to a quiet evening with my brother and Gigi, I wasn't disappointed to be greeted by the entire family. They were my lifeline when I felt hopeless. They were my support when I felt defeated. They were everything a punk-ass kid had needed to turn his life around and make something of himself from nothing.

CHAPTER 11
SAGE

"JAMES AND THOMAS, this is Sage, Austin's friend." Izzy had her hand on my arm, showing me off to the two men. "James is my husband, and Thomas, my brother," she explained.

"It's a pleasure to meet you," Thomas said, while James gave me a chin lift.

"Isn't she a pretty little thing for a soldier?" Izzy said, smiling brightly, eyes roaming over my face.

"Sailor," James corrected his wife, motioning toward the empty chairs at the dining room table. "Sit. Sit."

Izzy pulled out a chair and practically pushed me down. "Well, okay," I muttered, feeling so out of place.

"So, Sage, tell us about yourself. What made you want to join the military?" Thomas asked, grabbing the bottle of wine off the table and offering me a glass.

I nodded, smiling and thankful when I took the first sip. "My dad was military, and my mom worked for the government too. It felt right to follow in their footsteps."

"What did your mom do?" James asked, gazing at me over the top of the wineglass in his hand as he held Izzy's hand with the other.

"She was FBI."

"Impressive," James muttered.

"Thomas and James used to work for the DEA before they started their own security firm."

"What's your mom's name? Maybe we know her," Thomas asked.

I squirmed a little in my chair, not used to sharing personal information with strangers, but this was Austin's family. "Bobbie Hill."

James choked on his wine, and Thomas's mouth gaped open. "Bobbie is your mother?"

My eyes widened. "You know her?"

"Know her?" Thomas laughed. "We know both of your parents. Alex is a great guy, and Bobbie is a strong woman. They're some of the best people I know."

My mouth opened and closed as the words lodged in the back of my throat. "I can't believe you know my parents."

Thomas smiled, easing back in his chair. "We've

spoken to your father and mother a few times over the years, working different cases. They're a fountain of information when we're in need."

"There you are," Austin said as he walked into the dining room, taking the chair next to me. He studied me for a moment, his forehead furrowing. "You okay?"

"They know my parents." I tipped my head toward his uncles.

Austin jerked his head back as his eyes grew wider. "No shit. Small world."

"It's fate," Izzy added, smirking. "The world has a way of forcing people together."

I laughed nervously, twisting the stem of the wineglass between my fingers. "I guess we were always meant to be friends, then," I reminded him, along with everyone else around the table.

"Friends," Austin mumbled, agreeing with me. "My grandma and grandpa are dying to meet you. You up for it?"

"I would love to meet them." I couldn't wipe the smile off my face as he held out his hand and helped me up from my seat.

"Friends," Izzy whispered, laughing.

I followed Austin through the crowded house, not only bursting with people but also with chatter and love. There wasn't an empty chair in the place, and the floor was even covered with younger people sitting around talking.

"My sweet boy," an older woman said, holding out her arms as soon as we stepped near. "Let me see this beauty."

Austin positioned me in front of him, pushing me closer to the older woman. "Don't think she's blind. She's smart as a whip and hears everything," he said in my ear as she clasped my hands.

"Well, aren't you a sweet thing," she said softly, running her thumb across the top of my hand. "Thank you for your service, along with my grandson."

I smiled awkwardly, always unsure of what to say when someone would compliment me in that way. "You're welcome," I squeaked out, somehow still maintaining my weird smile.

"She's the best cook ever, Sage. You wait and see."

"You're staying for dinner Sunday, Austin?" she asked him, giving him the warmest smile.

"Yes, ma'am. I'll be there. I wouldn't miss it."

"Good, baby. I made all your favorites."

"You're the best, Grandma."

I stood there, watching their exchange, knowing he wasn't related to anyone in this house besides his brother through blood. But it didn't matter to these people. He was a member of the family and treated as such.

His entire demeanor had changed from the moment we'd stepped out of the car. There were layers to him, and I wanted to peel them back, exposing the real man underneath.

I'd misjudged him. Maybe he wasn't all bullshit and cocky flattery. Either way, I wanted to know who the real Austin Moore was and why I was drawn to him.

———————

The flames of the fire pit licked the air, casting shadows across Austin's face. "Thanks for a great night. We weren't expecting the entire family to be here."

His brother smiled as he sat across from us next to Gigi. "When they heard you were coming, they insisted."

"I miss easy nights like this," Austin said, staring at the fire. "The hardest part about military life is not being here with the family."

Gigi placed her hand over her heart like she was touched by his words. "We miss you too. Life's pretty boring without your cocky mouth around all the time."

Austin laughed. "Cocky? I was never cocky."

Gigi tilted her head, gawking at him. "I'm not sure cocky is even a strong enough word."

"You still are," I told Austin, throwing in my two cents. He wasn't over the top, but the man did think highly of himself.

Austin's gaze flickered to me, along with his sexy smile. "There's a difference between being cocky and self-assured. I know my value and abilities."

I rolled my eyes.

"You've always been full of shit," Pike told him, shaking his head.

Gigi covered her mouth and yawned. "Well, I'm tired and headed to bed. Austin, I made up your room and Sage's too. You know where they are and don't need a babysitter. Pike?"

"I'm coming, darlin'," he said, placing his empty beer bottle in the grass before standing. "Night."

"Night," Austin said, and so did I.

We sat in silence, watching them as they walked toward the house. Pike had his arm slung around her shoulders, holding her tight to his body.

"They're so perfect together," I whispered before they disappeared into the house.

Austin turned toward me, studying my face. "They fought it for a long time, but they were meant to be."

I blinked. "You believe in fate like Izzy?"

He gave me a small smile. "I wouldn't call it fate, but there was something at play. They met in Daytona and never thought they'd see each other again, and then bam! Pike shows up at her family's tattoo shop without realizing she'd be there."

"That sounds pretty much like fate." I laughed

softly, but my laughter died as Austin slid his chair closer to mine and touched my arm.

"If you think fate is real, then maybe we were meant to meet, and this moment was always supposed to happen."

I swallowed hard as the look on his face changed, and his gaze dipped to my mouth. "This moment?"

"This moment," he repeated as he leaned over and brought his mouth in line with mine.

I didn't move. I couldn't. All the air evaporated from my lungs, leaving me breathless. He'd kissed me before, but this time, he'd caught me completely off guard.

This was different. This was calculated.

My heart pounded as he stared into my eyes, coming closer. I held my breath, waiting for the moment his lips touched mine again. I closed my eyes, leaning forward, bringing my mouth to his.

I didn't have to wait long before his lips touched mine, sending shock waves of pleasure throughout my body. His mouth was soft, but the kiss was hard.

He moved his hand to my face, cupping my cheek as I snaked my arms around his neck. When his tongue swept across my bottom lip, I opened to him, taking what he had to give.

Time stood still, and the crackling of the fire in front of us grew faint, almost disappearing. Only the sounds of our harsh breaths and needy pants were audible.

When he pulled away, I stayed motionless, my lips still puckered and my eyes closed.

"Let's go inside," he said as I opened my eyes.

"Okay," I whispered.

My insides were a jumbled mess as I took his hand, letting him lead me toward the house. Would I sleep with him? Did he want to sleep with me? There were so many questions running through my mind as we made our way up the stairs to the line of closed doors to various bedrooms.

He stopped us in front of the third door, gripping my hand. "Here's your room. I'll be right next door if you need anything."

I gaped at him but quickly masked the expression.

He wasn't going to sleep with me?

I thought… Hell, after the kiss we'd had outside, I thought for sure he wanted more.

"Thank you," I replied, unsure of what to do or say.

Did I want him to leave?

I knew we only had a few more days together, and then I'd never see him again. I already liked him way more than I wanted, and it would be dangerous to my heart to let myself fall even further.

"You can come in if you want," I blurted, ignoring my inner voice trying to warn me away from him.

He squeezed my fingers as his eyes roamed my face. "Only if you want me to."

I gulped, unsure exactly what I wanted. "I do," I said without another moment's hesitation, sounding surprisingly sure of myself, which I wasn't.

"We can just talk."

I raised an eyebrow, not really wanting to talk all night, but there was one thing I could do with him for hours. "And kiss?"

He laughed softly, his blue eyes sparkling. "And kiss."

My hand moved to the knob, opening the door, and I pulled him inside. I didn't even look around the room. I was too busy staring at Austin, his handsome face, and the hungry look in his eyes.

We weren't even five steps inside the room before he kicked the door closed with one foot and grabbed me around the waist with his hands, planting his lips on mine. There was no hesitation as our bodies collided and our mouths moved together.

This time, I didn't keep my hands around his shoulders. I let them roam his body, sweeping over the hard planes of his stomach and his firm pecs. He was nothing but mouthwatering muscle, without an ounce of fat anywhere on his body. Even as I moved my hands to his back, sliding them down to his ass, I was met with two ass cheeks so hard they were like granite.

"Damn," I whispered against his lips, dragging my hands up to his back. "You're so..." The words died in my throat as his lips glided to my neck.

I tilted my head to the side, letting him taste my flesh as I dug my fingernails into the taut skin of his sides. Just as I was starting to pant, Austin's lips were gone.

"What are you doing?"

He licked his lips, smiling ruefully. "I can't."

I drew my eyebrows down, confused. "You can't what?"

"We shouldn't do this. After this weekend, I'll be gone, and you'll be here. The last thing I want to do is break your heart."

I jerked my head back, trying not to slap him in his crazy-ass mouth. "You're worried about breaking my heart?"

He nodded with the smirk still firmly planted on his sexy lips.

"Listen, Austin. You're hot and kind of pretty, but just because we have sex doesn't mean I'm going to be begging for you to put a ring on it."

"Darlin'," he murmured, reaching out to cup my cheek. "After one night with me, no other man will do."

"You are so full of it." I shook my head, grabbing his shirt and pulling him closer. "Maybe you're not man enough to handle me, or maybe, just maybe, you're the one falling for me. Are you scared of falling for me, Austin?" I challenged him, knowing full well he was the type of man who never liked to admit anything scared him.

"I'm not scared of you, Dynasty."

"Then prove it." I stared into his blue eyes, waiting for him to let down his guard and kiss me.

He stared back, eyes blazing with desire and the fear he tried so hard to hide and deny.

It only took a minute before his lips crashed down on mine again and the pull we'd tried so hard to resist won out.

In two days when we said goodbye, would I regret not walking away sooner?

CHAPTER 12
AUSTIN

"YOU SURE YOU want to do this?"

Sage gazed up at me, fear filling her eyes. "I do."

I raised an eyebrow, not buying her words. "I won't think you're a chicken for backing out."

She lifted her chin defiantly. "I'm not backing out." Sage lifted her arm and jabbed me square in the chest. "Maybe it's you who wants to back out."

I laughed, grabbing her wrist. "Darlin', I've never been afraid of a little needle."

"Aren't they so cute together?" Gigi asked Pike, standing off to the side inside the Inked waiting room.

We both turned, staring at them.

"Yeah, babe. Whatever you say," he told her as he brushed his lips against her forehead. "We ready to do this?"

Sage nodded and stalked away from me, heading

toward Gigi. "Never been more ready for anything in my life."

I shook my head, unable to wipe the dumb smile off my face. Pike stared at me, not moving, just watching as the two women disappeared inside Gigi's room.

"You got it bad, brother. Really bad."

I stiffened, narrowing my eyes. "I do not."

"Maybe you don't see it now, but next week, when you're gone, you're not going to be able to get her out of your head."

"I've had plenty of women." I shrugged, moving across the waiting room toward my brother. "What's one more?"

He placed his hand on my shoulder, squeezing. "I've seen you with plenty of women, but none have your balls so locked up in a vise like this one. You can deny shit all you want, but there's something different about her and the way you talk to her."

I looked him right in the eye, straightening my posture. "I'm not denying she's great. I'm not even going to say I don't like her, but we're friends and will probably always be friends. Nothing more."

Pike laughed, releasing his grip on me. "Whatever you say. You ready for a few hours of pain?"

"I've already had a lifetime. What's a little more?"

My brother rolled his eyes. "You've always been dramatic. How do your military buddies put up with your shit?"

I followed him into his room, kicking off my boots as soon as I entered because I was going to be comfortable, or at least as much as I could be. "They're no better. If you think I'm dramatic, you should meet the others."

"Maybe I will. Gigi keeps talking about visiting you in California soon."

"I'd love that."

"Me too." He motioned for me to sit, and I did, waiting as he moved around the room, grabbing a pair of gloves. "We still doing this on your stomach?"

"Still the stomach." I lifted my shirt over my head, exposing the very little bit of skin I had left untouched.

"You're running out of room."

I lay down on the table, trying to make myself comfortable on the thin cushion. "Pot meet kettle."

Pike laughed as he settled in next to me, having already prepared everything before we arrived. "So, tell me, are you still happy you joined the service? I've always felt like shit that you left us."

"Pike, don't ever feel like shit about me joining up and leaving home. I needed to do something on my own. Something without the help of others. Something without my past following me. You know?"

He nodded, reaching for the tattoo gun. "I do know. It's why I left home, leaving all the bullshit behind. I wanted something that was just mine.

Something I wasn't given in Tennessee just for being a Moore."

I tucked my hands behind my head, taking in slow breaths, knowing over the next few hours, my skin would feel like hot coals were being dragged across it repeatedly. "I'm proud of myself and everything I've achieved, for the first time in my life. It wasn't about leaving you behind but finding out who I was."

He smiled down at me as he sat at my side. "I'm proud of you, too."

I closed my eyes, trying not to let my emotions get the better of me. "That means more than you'll ever know."

Although I had the Gallos, Pike was my only blood relative still alive besides my father. Before Pike left home when I was a little kid, we were as close as any siblings could be with our age difference. My father was never one to say he was proud of me, no matter what I'd accomplished, but hearing those words from my brother meant more than any praise I could've received from anyone else in the world.

"Now, let's get this shit over with so we can get out of here and spend the night with our girls."

I peered down my body at him.

"I know. I know. She's not your girl," he said quickly before I could say the words. "But she will be."

"Why do you keep saying that?"

"You know how I met Gigi, yeah?"

"I do."

He wet my stomach before placing the design on my skin, running his hand across the paper. "I never thought we would be more. When she left me there in the hotel, I figured it was a fun week. I thought just like you." He pulled the paper away from my stomach and smacked my leg with a mirror. "This where you want it?"

I took the mirror from his hands, looking at the reflection of my stomach. "Looks perfect."

"Then we're doing this."

"We are."

"If you hadn't have run into her here, you wouldn't ever have seen her again, though, brother. Remember that."

"I looked for her. I tried to find some leads on her, but I had nothing. I had a name and a wrong city. She lied to me."

"Sounds like she was deeply in love with you." I snickered.

He lifted the tattoo gun, glaring down at me. "I got her in the end, didn't I?"

"Dumb luck and you're relentless when you want something."

"You never really know exactly what you want until it's gone. You'll see. I give you a week in California before she's the only thing you can think of."

"She's being deployed soon. She'll be out of the country for months."

"Even better." He smiled.

I growled as the needle touched my skin, always forgetting the pain, especially on the tender skin of my abdomen.

"You'll have plenty of time to pine for her."

"You're an asshole."

"It's genetic." He laughed.

I missed this easiness with my brother.

I missed home.

I missed our family, the new family who made me feel like I had always been with them.

I had no regrets about joining the military. It was my life. My calling. My world. I was good at my job. I thrived under the pressure and danger. But I was never completely whole unless I was here. Maybe that was why I didn't come back often. Being here reminded me of the things I was missing. The family dinners. The birthdays. The cookouts. The holidays. But I'd be back. I'd be a better version of myself and the man I wanted to become.

Sage lay next to me, our hands touching. "The stars are so beautiful here."

"It's the best thing about living in the middle of

nowhere, but this is nothing compared to what you'll see on deployment."

She turned her head, drawing my attention. "It's dark out there, isn't it?"

"It's the blackest black you'll ever experience. You never realize how much light there is here, even now, until you're in the middle of the ocean."

She sighed, blinking slowly. "I don't know if I'm ready for everything."

I tangled my fingers with hers, knowing what she was feeling. "It's scary at first, but you'll fall into a routine after a week or so. I'm not saying it won't suck, because it will, but you'll make it through with flying colors."

She squeezed my fingers, giving me a faint smile. "What's the worst part of it?"

I rolled on my side, peering down at her. "The worst part is your downtime. You're going to be bored. Fill up your e-reader, download some movies, and bring other things to keep yourself occupied. There will be times when you won't have internet at all. Long periods of time. But back in the day, people had no connection with home except letters."

"I don't think I could've made it with only letters."

"Mail delivery is still the most exciting day on the ship. Everyone runs on deck to see what they got. I lived for those days."

"Did you get a lot of packages?"

"I used to get so many things it was crazy.

Sometimes, we wouldn't get anything for a month, and then, bam, dozens of packages. You'll see."

She peered down at the blanket between us. "Will you write to me?" she asked, still not bringing her gaze back to mine. "I could use your wisdom and support. Someone besides my dad being my cheerleader from the side. Someone I could share my fears or even successes with who will be honest with me and who I can be honest with too."

I placed my fingers under her chin, bringing her gaze back to me in the starlight. "I'll write to you, darlin'. You can tell me anything, and I'll never judge you."

She smiled and let out a relieved breath. "Thank you, Austin. That means a lot to me."

"You can text me too. You'll be able to use some apps at sea when you're not under a blackout. Reach out to me anytime, and I'll reply as soon as I can." I swept my finger across her face underneath her lips, wanting nothing more than to kiss her again.

"You're always on the move, aren't you?"

"Not always, but I'm not at base as much as I'd like to be."

"I promise not to bother you too much."

I tightened my fingers on her chin. "Darlin', you could never be a bother. When you need me, I'll be there for you."

She lifted her arm, resting her hand on my bicep. "Why are you so great to me?"

"Why wouldn't I be nice to you?"

She shrugged a shoulder, gripping my arm tighter. "I don't know. I figured you were only being nice to get into my pants."

I laughed, shaking my head. "I won't lie. I did want in your pants, but that's not why I was nice."

"Did?" She quirked a brown eyebrow, smiling.

"Do," I corrected my statement. "But that's not why I'm nice. I like you, Sage. I like you more than any other woman I've ever spent time with. God, I sound like such a pussy saying those words, but I'm drawn to you."

She moved her hand up my arm to my shoulder, giving me a closer look at her new ink. The words *do not go gentle into that good night. rage, rage against the dying of the light* were barely visible in black ink on the underside of her forearm, hidden by the bandages. "I'm drawn to you too," she whispered, like it was a secret neither one of us wanted to admit.

Using my weight, I pushed her onto her back, covering her upper body with mine. "I'm going to kiss you, Sage."

"Okay," she whispered, staring up at me with her green eyes flickering under the stars.

"I want to make love to you," I replied, having never said those words to anyone else in my life. Sure, I'd wanted to fuck plenty of women in my time, but never anything tender and meaningful like I did with her in that moment.

"Out in the open?"

"Who's around?" I asked, looking up and into the darkness. "I can't see ten feet from us, and no one can see us either."

She bit her lip and tilted her head, looking around the dark field. "That's dangerous, Austin."

"Darlin', sometimes you need a little danger to remember how sweet life really is."

Her face softened as I brushed a few hairs away from her cheek. "You're going to break my heart, aren't you?" she asked.

"Who says you're not going to break mine?" I asked her before leaning in, placing my lips on hers.

Consequences be damned. I wanted her, and nothing else mattered in that moment. I'd rather have a little heartache than live with the regret of never being with her.

She moved her hands down my arms to my abs, sliding them underneath my shirt. I flinched as her nails touched the edges of the protective bandage my brother had lectured me about keeping clean. She fisted the material of my shirt, pushing it up my back as I pulled my lips away from hers to allow her to remove it.

"You're really pretty," she whispered as her hungry eyes roamed down my chest.

"There's nothing in this world more beautiful than you, Sage."

She smiled up at me, and our eyes locked. "You really know what to say to make a girl feel wanted."

"I've never wanted anyone or anything more," I admitted, gripping her hip with one hand as I took her lips again.

Her fingers found their way to the nape of my neck, her nails digging into my skin just enough to bite. I nipped at her plump lips, moaning every time she dipped her tongue into my mouth, circling mine.

I lowered my torso onto hers, immediately pulling back when pain radiated from my stomach. "Fuck," I hissed, hating my dumb ass for the tattoo.

"Maybe we should wait," she murmured against my lips. "Maybe we're rushing this."

I leaned forward, resting my forehead against hers. "I've never been good at waiting, Dynasty."

"I don't know if I can do this and then say goodbye to you, Austin. I'm not the type of girl that sleeps around. Giving myself to you is a big step, and I don't want to ruin our friendship and whatever else this is or will be."

I knew she was right, but my dick didn't seem to agree. I rolled onto my back, pulling her with me and tucking her against me. "We can wait," I said, sucking in a breath, trying to get my heart to stop pounding and my dick to calm down too.

"Are you mad?" she whispered into the darkness.

"For what?"

"Are you mad if we don't have sex?"

I ran my fingers through her hair as it spilled down her back. "I could never be mad about something as important as this. Never."

She placed her hand on my chest, tipping her head back to look at me. "Thank you."

I kissed her forehead, letting my lips linger on her skin. "Thank you for coming home with me."

"I love it here. I love your family."

"They loved having you here too."

"Austin," she whispered.

"Yeah, darlin'?"

"Do you think we'll see each other again after this weekend?"

I flattened my palm against her back, holding her tighter. "I sure as hell hope so."

CHAPTER 13
SAGE

I'D HAD moments of regret in my life. Everyone had something they wished they'd never done or said. But I could never imagine Austin Moore being thrown into the regrets column. He'd been nothing but kind and even sweet at times, something I never would've expected when we first met.

I crossed my legs, placing my hand on my stomach as it growled for the third time in less than five minutes. The house smelled like heaven. When he said his grandmother was a good cook and we'd get a great meal out of the trip, I hadn't expected something like this. There were dozens of bowls and pots filled with different sauces, pastas, lasagna, sausage, meatballs, and things I'd only seen in restaurants.

"I hope you're hungry," Izzy said as she stood

near me, James practically glued to her. "Ma's been cooking all day."

"She didn't have to go to all this trouble," I told her, my eyes moving across the kitchen counter where there wasn't a spot not filled by something to eat. "It's a lot of work for someone her age."

Izzy's eyebrows shot up. "Her age?" She laughed, covering her mouth.

"You better not let her hear you say that," Austin whispered at my side. "Gram may be older, but she can whip everyone's ass in this room with a single glance."

"Is she like a mental ninja?" I chuckled, finding my sense of humor funny, but no one else laughed.

He placed his hand on my leg, squeezing my knee. "She's the queen bee and the one in the family you don't cross."

I slid my hand up to my chest. "I wasn't crossing her. I was just saying…"

He lowered his head, getting close to me. "She's older. We know it. She knows it. But for the love of God, do not tell her that."

"What are you talking about?" his grandmother said as she walked into the living room, standing next to Izzy and James. "It got quiet in here real quick."

"We're just talking about how hungry we are," Austin said, smiling up at the beautiful older woman. "I've been waiting for this meal for a year."

The kind woman, the one he called his gram even though they weren't related, smiled down at him with so much admiration and love. "I cooked all your favorites, baby."

"You spoil me," he told her, reaching for her hand and kissing the back. "I've missed you the most."

She laughed and then swatted his hand away from hers. "You're smooth, but a liar too."

He chuckled, shaking his head as she marched back into the kitchen, towel thrown over her shoulder.

Izzy wrapped her arms around her middle across James's where he held her. "She has your number, Austin. Always has."

"She loves me." He beamed.

"We all do for some odd reason." Izzy turned her head, gazing up at her handsome husband. "Is the other surprise here yet?"

She looked at him like he was the only man on earth. The same way my mother stared at my father. There was nothing but love between them, and it showed to everyone who was looking.

"Any minute, Iz. Everything's in place."

The smile was still on her face when she turned back to face us. "The day is going to be even better."

I peered over at Austin, getting a shrug in response.

"Fuck if I know."

Then there was a knock on the front door, and Izzy was out of James's arms, screaming, "I'll get it!" as she ran to answer, with James stalking behind her.

"Those two are always up to something," Gigi said to me as she sat between Pike's legs on the floor. "Never trust them."

"Oh boy," I whispered, holding my stomach again out of hunger and a little bit of fear.

"They're not mean, but you never know what's going to happen when Izzy makes a plan."

"Great," I muttered. "Well, at least it's not an assassin coming to get us all."

Austin laughed, his hand still on my knee. I leaned to the right, resting my side against his. We were comfortable together, something I'd never experienced with anyone else before. Not this level of comfort so quickly, and never without a deep physical relationship.

"Look who came to visit," Izzy said, marching into the living room with James's tall frame behind her.

Austin and I glanced up, me blinking because I couldn't see anyone else except the two of them, and I didn't know anyone else around here.

But then they stepped to the side, and a man I'd never expected to see here, or at least not for a long time, stood in the middle of the Gallos' living room.

"Daddy?" I gasped, jumping up from the couch and running toward my dad like I hadn't seen him in years.

Two days ago, we'd said our goodbyes. Two days ago, I'd cried, not knowing when I'd see him again.

His arms were around me before I was close enough to wrap mine around him. "Hey, sweetheart. James called, and I was still in Florida. I took a chopper down here to visit and share a meal before heading back to Virginia. I couldn't leave without seeing you again."

Tears formed in my eyes as I hugged my dad, happy to see him and completely surprised. "I just can't believe you're here." My dad kissed the top of my head before I pulled away, wiping at my eyes. "I'm sure you were busy."

"Never too busy for you." My dad's eyes moved to Austin, giving him a quick nod. "I heard this was the one meal I couldn't miss or I'd regret it for the rest of my life."

I laughed, having been told the same thing. "I'm happy you're here, Dad."

"Never imagined I'd get a call from James about something other than business, but this was a welcome surprise."

I smiled up at him, beaming with pride. "I didn't know you had ties to Austin's family."

"I found out yesterday when I got the report on Austin, but you didn't tell me you were going home with him."

I glanced down, hiding my eyes. "Well." I shrugged. "I didn't think it was important."

"You're grown, Sage. You can do what you want. You know what's safe and what isn't. I trust you and your judgment."

I lifted my head, peering up at my dad. "I'm always safe."

"I taught you how to protect yourself. I'm sure if Austin was an asshole, you'd deal with him."

I laughed. "I may have shown him a few moves already."

My dad's eyebrows furrowed as his eyes darted to Austin. "You did?"

"I swear I did nothing. We were sparring," Austin replied with his hands in the air. "I never touched her."

"Alex, want a drink?" James asked, changing the subject.

Dad nodded. "I'll take a beer if you have it."

"Join me on the lanai for a chat too." James motioned toward the sliding glass doors off the living room. "I'll grab the beers. Thomas will be joining us."

That meant the meeting wasn't entirely about me. At least not for James and Thomas, but none of that mattered because my dad was here, and I'd get to spend a little more time with him before we'd have to say goodbye again.

My dad touched my back. "You okay with that?"

I nodded. "Of course. I'll be fine." I lifted up on my toes and kissed my dad's cheek. "I kind of love this family," I whispered. "They're great people."

My dad smiled down at me. "I've known James and Thomas for almost as long as you've been alive, and yes, sweetheart, they're some of the best people."

"How much longer until dinner, Ma?" James asked his mother-in-law.

"Twenty minutes, so make it snappy," she told him, getting a nod in return.

"I love when she bosses him around," Gigi said as she came to stand next to me. "He's always so bossy with everyone else, and there's nothing more rewarding than seeing him get a little taste of his own medicine."

I laughed, knowing how she felt. "My dad's crazy bossy too. It's part of the male DNA."

"The women in our family are fierce too, and from what I can tell, you fit right in."

I turned, gawking at her. "We're not dating, Gigi."

She chuckled, shaking her head. "Not yet."

I blinked with my mouth still hanging open.

"I see how he looks at you. It's the same way his brother looked at me."

"It's not—"

"We'll see who's right," she told me before walking off.

I stood there, watching her hair sway as she sauntered back to Pike and made herself comfortable between his legs again.

"You okay?" Austin asked as I stayed frozen.

I didn't answer.

He touched my shoulder, brushing my hair back. "Sage, you okay?" he repeated.

"I'm great," I whispered, blinking through the haze. "We were just having a little girl talk."

"Oh boy," he muttered. "Those are never good."

I gazed up at him, pushing away all the questions going through my mind. "What time are we heading back?" I asked, wondering how long we had to enjoy his family and my father.

"Not for a few hours. You don't have to be at the ship tonight, do you?"

I shook my head, clearing it. "Duty isn't until morning."

"I'll have you back in plenty of time to get some shut-eye."

"Thanks, Austin."

He touched my cheek, brushing his fingertips across my skin. "I'm the one who should be thanking you for coming here with me this weekend. It wouldn't have been the same without you."

I gazed into his eyes, seeing the way he studied me, knowing he looked at me like Pike stared at Gigi. "I'll never forget this weekend. Never."

He moved his fingers to my chin, and I held my breath, thinking he was going to kiss me. "Me either, darlin'," he whispered before dropping his hand from my face.

Every time he called me darlin', my insides would go all squishy. I'd never admit it, though. Not to him —or anyone else, for that matter. But it still happened. Add in the way he looked at me, how he touched me, and I was an absolute goner.

Three hours later, we stood in the front yard, hugging and saying our goodbyes. There wasn't a person in the family who hadn't welcomed me with open arms or who didn't hug me tightly when saying goodbye.

"Don't be a stranger," Gigi said to me before she let me go. "You have my number now. Keep in touch, and the next time you need a tattoo, I'm a quick drive away. You're always welcome in our home too."

I smiled as my vision blurred. I wouldn't cry. I wouldn't cry because I had to say goodbye to these wonderful people I'd only known for a few short days.

"I'll call," I whispered, holding on to her arms for a moment longer than I should have.

"You'll be back," she said, winking. "Mark my words."

I laughed, finally letting her go. "You're crazy."

"I know the Moore men better than anyone else in the world, and I'm never wrong."

"You're full of shit," Pike said, throwing his arm around her shoulder. "She's wrong a lot. Don't listen to a word she says."

Gigi craned her neck, glaring up at her man. "So, Austin isn't crazy for Sage?"

Pike winced. "Okay, so maybe you're right sometimes."

Gigi beamed. "See?" she said, turning back toward me. "I told you."

"Sage!" Austin yelled from the driveway, where he stood with my father. "Ready?"

"Bye." I waved to Gigi and Pike, unable to wipe the dumb smile off my face. "Thanks for everything."

"Take care of that tat," Gigi said as I walked away, and I waved to the rest of the family as their gazes moved between Austin and me.

"I'll give you two a moment," Austin said, stepping away from my father and me.

My father nodded at him, waiting for him to leave us before speaking. He wrapped his big arms around my body, holding me tighter than he had in years. "I won't see you before deployment."

"I know," I muttered into the soft cotton fabric of his T-shirt.

"Be careful out there, and let us know you're okay when you can."

"I will."

He held me tighter. "Maybe you should've joined the air force."

"Dad," I groaned into his chest. "Stop. I'll be fine."

"Do you like this man?"

I pulled away slightly, leaning back so I could see my dad's face. "What?"

"Do you like Austin?"

I blinked, thrown off by the question and quick change of topic. "He's nice."

He raised an eyebrow, peering down at me with the fatherly look I'd always hated. "You're not answering my question."

"I like him," I admitted, petrified my dad would warn me away from him.

Austin was older. He was military and not just navy, but a SEAL. My father knew the dangers of such work and the life.

"But," I added before my dad could say anything else, "we're only friends."

"You keep saying that. It's like you have an answer ready for all things. I've known you since you took your first breath, baby. If you like the man, don't let your stubbornness or the distance get in the way of getting what you want."

I opened my mouth and shut it again when I wasn't sure what to say.

"All I want is for you to be happy."

"I am happy, Dad."

He grabbed me by the arms, staring at me. "I am lucky to be your dad."

"I'm lucky you're my father."

If I hadn't known any better, I'd have thought my dad had the thinnest layer of tears in his eyes. "You better go," he said before looking over his shoulder to where Austin stood off to the side, talking to Pike. "She's ready."

I rolled my eyes. "Maybe I wasn't."

"You were. I have to go. The chopper is waiting for me to head back to Virginia."

I gave him one last squeeze and a kiss. "I love you."

He touched my face, smiling at me. "Love you too."

"Do you need a ride?" Austin asked my father.

"James is taking me to the airport. You two head back. I want you there before sundown."

"Yes, sir," Austin said, holding out his hand to shake my dad's.

My father didn't even hesitate, sliding his palm against Austin's. "Thanks for being there for my daughter."

I gawked at them both. My father had never liked any man I'd ever brought around him. Never. It didn't matter how good their family was, how wonderful they were as a person, or how many accomplishments they had. But Austin was different. Austin was cut from the same cloth, part of the same brotherhood as my father. He was a SEAL.

"Whenever she needs me, I'll be there," Austin told him.

"I'm right here," I reminded them both, glaring at them.

Dad laughed. "Text me when you get back to base."

I rolled my eyes, getting a growl from my father.

"Okay. A text it is," I mumbled.

"Let's hit it, Dynasty."

"I'm driving," I told him, taking the keys from his hands. "You drive like a wild man."

Austin threw up his hands as he walked to the passenger door. "I have no problems giving up control."

"Bye!" various members of the Gallo family yelled out as I climbed in next to Austin.

I waved just as Austin did.

"I love your family."

"Me too," he said as a quick flash of sadness passed across his face. "This is the hardest part of military life, but we sacrifice to keep them safe and know that the distance isn't forever."

"We do." I placed the key in the ignition, turning on the engine. "Now, buckle up, big boy. It's going to be a long ride."

"A slow ride," he muttered, reaching for his seat belt.

"My mom taught me how to drive, and she does nothing slow. I'm careful, but we're going to beat your time record here."

"Then why are you driving if you're going to drive worse?"

I laughed, gripping the wheel. "I didn't say worse.

I said safer. Did I tell you about how I worked at a racetrack for a summer?"

Austin's face paled. "Wait! I don't think this is a good idea."

I chuckled, revving the engine before taking off as he squealed like a baby.

CHAPTER 14
AUSTIN

"SO, THIS IS IT?" Sage asked as she held on to my shirt. "You have to leave now?"

I nodded, stroking the skin on her arm. "I've been called back early since my meetings are over. I have to be in California by oh-eight-hundred."

"I was hoping we'd…"

"Me too, darlin'." I brushed a few hairs behind her ear. "Although we had all weekend, it didn't feel like enough time."

"Maybe we'll meet again," she whispered.

"I never know where I'll be in the world and when, but I'm sure our paths will cross again."

I'd never had a problem saying goodbye to a woman, but there was something about Sage that made it damn near impossible. The last thing I wanted to do was leave, especially since I was just getting to know her better. I always had a good time when I went home, but being with her had only made things better.

"Sure," she muttered, not sounding convinced. "It's possible. I mean, anything is, right?"

I gazed down at her, holding her face in my palm as she leaned into my touch. "In a few months, you'll forget all about me."

"I will not."

"You will. You'll fall for someone on your ship after being stuck at sea with them for what feels like forever."

"Every time I look up at the stars, I'll think of you."

"I'll do the same."

She clutched my shirt tighter. "This really sucks, you know?"

I nodded, feeling the warmth of her hand through my shirt. "It does, but I don't regret meeting you. I don't regret a minute we spent together."

"Not even that we didn't…" She waggled her eyebrows.

I smiled, biting my lip. God, I wanted her so badly, but there was no time. I'd blown my chance now. But it was probably for the better. Saying goodbye would be so much harder for both of us if we had. "No regrets."

"Kiss me one last time before you go," she pleaded, her green eyes blazing in the dim lighting outside her building.

I tightened my fingers behind her neck. "Are you sure?"

"I wouldn't ask if I weren't sure. This kiss has to get me through a long deployment."

"That's a lot of pressure, darlin'."

She leaned forward, pressing her chest against mine. "I'm sure you've had more pressure than a little kiss."

I snaked my other arm around her back, digging my fingers into the softness of her side. "I don't do anything little."

She smirked, knowing she was getting the reaction she wanted from me. "Prove it."

I did what any man being challenged would do. I pulled her closer, smashing our bodies together before taking her lips, hard and demanding. She felt so right in my arms, like she was always meant to be there and I was made to hold her.

Moans slipped from her lips as her hands slid up my arms to my shoulders, holding me tight. Then her fingers toyed with the skin at the nape of my neck, and goose bumps broke out across my skin as if they were reaching for more of her touch.

I didn't know how long we stood there with our arms wrapped around each other, lips locked, breathing each other in. Time seemed to stand still as I tried to memorize the sounds, smells, and taste of Sage to get me through many lonely nights ahead.

"Stop," she whispered against my lips, breaking the moment. "I can't..."

"I'm sorry," I breathed heavily, resting my forehead against hers, wishing we could be so much more. "This wasn't a good idea."

"No. No," she said before sighing. "I want more than we can have. I don't like admitting that either, Austin. It makes me feel weak."

I splayed my hand across her back, holding on to her as long as I could. "You're not weak. You're one of the strongest women I know."

"You make me feel weak," she admitted, looking down.

"You make me weak," I told her, saying the words I never thought I'd say before meeting her. Vulnerability wasn't something I'd ever been comfortable with, and I was definitely not used to sharing my feelings with others. That was a part of my heartless father I'd carried with me for far too long.

She moved her hands to my front, flattening her palms against my chest over my rapidly beating heart. "You better go. This isn't going to get any easier, and we're only delaying the inevitable."

I covered her fingers with my hands, holding her. "Don't forget me too fast."

She smiled softly. "You're pretty unforgettable."

"Finally, you admit it," I said smugly, smirking.

"You're an asshole, but the best kind." She took a

step back, her hand slipping out from underneath mine. Our eyes were locked as she stepped farther back, putting more space between us. "Text me sometime if you remember who I am when you get back to the hot babes in Cali."

I shook my head, laughing quietly. "No one compares to you, Sage."

Her smile widened. "You're a good liar sometimes, Han, but only sometimes."

"Good—"

"Don't say it. I'm shit at goodbyes. This isn't goodbye. It can't be," she said from across the parking lot.

I waved, swallowing down any more words I wanted to say. There was nothing that could make either of us feel better. There was nothing we could do to change our circumstances. We were property of the United States government. Our lives weren't our own…at least not for now.

When she got to her front door, she turned to face me, giving me one final glance over her shoulder. I smiled at her, memorizing every inch of her body and the way the setting sun danced across her beautiful face.

A sad smile and a moment later, she was gone.

CHAPTER 15
SAGE

Seven Months Later

AFTER MONTHS AT SEA, every inch of my body was buzzing as we sailed into the harbor, waiting to anchor. We stood along the deck, lining the railing in our uniforms, searching for familiar faces in the crowd gathered at the water's edge, as they did the same.

"You ready for this?" Blondie asked as he stood by my side.

"Ready isn't even the right word. I feel like we've been gone an eternity."

"The longest seven months of my life."

"You're not lying," I replied as I squinted, trying to find my parents and little brother among the people.

"At least you're first off. You got lucky, you know. That spot should've been mine."

He was referring to the competition we'd had on board for the sailor to be first off to greet their family. I'd won by the slimmest of margins, beating Blondie and a few others, but just barely.

"Maybe you should've tried harder." I smirked.

"I'm going to be standing in line for hours while you'll already be sipping a cold beer."

"Sucks to be you." I chuckled for a second before sobering, not wanting to get my ass chewed out by an officer.

An hour later, our ship was tethered to the pier, and sailors were milling around the deck, waiting to be released. I saluted the commanding officer, being the first one down the gangway from my group. I was halfway down when I saw my father, mother, and Sawyer standing straight ahead, smiles so damn big on their faces.

I ran to my parents, unable to walk slowly and play it cool. I threw myself into their waiting arms, forgetting about Sawyer for a second because...well, he was Sawyer.

"We missed you," Mom said, kissing my cheek.

"You look good, kid," Dad added, staring at me as if he'd never really looked at me before.

"God, we were so worried," Mom told me. "I hated not knowing where you were."

"I'm fine. It wasn't that bad," I told them because

nothing eventful had happened the entire time. And besides being boring as hell, it wasn't the worst thing I could've experienced.

I'd seen a few countries, but only for a short time, mostly spending time on their base rather than exploring. Join the navy and see the world is what they told you, but you saw way more water than you saw land or other cultures.

"Did you get to shoot the big gun?" Sawyer asked as he stood next to my father, looking so much like him.

"I shot the big gun, Sawyer."

"Right on." He smiled, giving me a chin lift like he respected that.

The kid played too many video games and his brain was fried, but I knew he'd be in my shoes in a few years. He wanted to follow in Dad's footsteps more than I did. He'd probably end up a SEAL too, something I would never do.

"Hungry?" Dad asked, taking my duffel bag from my hands. "We thought we could grab something to eat before giving you the night to relax."

"Oh." I glanced around, hoping to see someone else, but finding no other familiar faces. "I thought maybe…"

"You thought Austin would be here?" Mom asked, having heard all about him every time we talked while I was gone.

Austin hadn't disappeared after we'd said goodbye

in the parking lot of my building. We wrote letters, something I only did with my parents. He sent me packages filled with snacks, candy, and a few books. We texted when we could and exchanged photos whenever possible. He never stopped flirting with me, and I did the same. Our relationship was a weird mix of pen pal and promise.

"I thought maybe he would be, but I guess I was wrong." I kicked my boots against the cement, annoyed and disappointed.

"He was out on assignment, sweetheart. It was last minute. He called me a few days ago and told me to tell you he was sorry he couldn't be here," Dad explained.

"I understand," I said, sounding so whiny, I wanted to kick my own ass.

I knew how his job worked. He could be called away at any minute and sent anywhere in the world. I knew it from my father, my mother, and through the limited information Austin had been able to share with me over the last seven months.

Out of the two of us, he was the only one seeing the world. I saw water and more water, while he was sent to far-off places—mostly dumps, as he'd called them—and I was stuck on a ship.

My mother gave my father a weird look before it quickly disappeared. She looped her arm through mine, moving me away from the gangway. "What do you want to eat, baby? A burger?"

"A big fat steak, Mom." I smiled at her, having missed her so crazy much. "Real mashed potatoes too."

"Whatever your heart desires," she said, laughing. "I know the food aboard is awful. A girl can only eat so many salads."

"Can I stop at home first to change and shower?"

"Your father is hungry. Can you wait on the shower?" My mom shot my dad another quick look. "You know how he gets when he's hungry."

"I'm already feeling cranky," Dad added, throwing an arm around Sawyer as he carried my duffel.

"Okay." I shrugged with a sigh, resigned that even though it was my day, I wasn't going to get my way.

It was fine. When I did finally make it home, I was going to soak in the bathtub for hours before collapsing into my bed and spreading out after being stuck in a tiny rack for months on end.

My legs wobbled a little as we walked toward the parking lot. After a solid month without stepping foot on land, I still felt like the ground was swaying underneath me like it had on the ship.

"You okay?" Mom whispered to me so my dad and Sawyer couldn't hear.

"I'm fine. Just getting my sea legs under control."

"I can imagine. Even after being on a cruise ship for a few days, I can't walk right for a few minutes when we port."

"Mom, can I ask you something?"

She turned, her hair blowing in the wind, looking every bit as beautiful as she always had. "You know you can ask me anything."

"When did you know Daddy was the one?"

She thought for a second, studying my face. "I'm still not convinced he is." She laughed.

"Mom." I giggled, snuggling into her. "You know you're crazy about the man."

"Sometimes, but he's also a pain in the ass."

"Like you're so easy."

"I am," she scoffed. "Why do you ask?"

"Just wondering," I lied.

"Wait." She stopped walking and turned her head toward me. "Do you think Austin is the one?"

"What?" My eyes widened. "No. That's crazy."

She eyed me for a second, always able to read me, which was part of her mom magic and FBI voodoo. "Are you sure?"

"Of course," I said quickly, starting to walk toward the cars again. "Man, I'm so hungry, I could eat the entire cow."

"Uh-huh," Mom muttered, but thankfully, she let the topic go.

———

Three hours later, I climbed out of the bathtub, exhausted after one of the longest days I'd had in months. I'd texted Austin numerous times while I soaked, but he didn't answer. He was probably halfway across the world, knee-deep in some crazy shit, and couldn't respond, but it still bothered me.

I toweled off, wrapping myself in my softest robe, happy to have something against my skin that wasn't government-issued and scratchy as hell. I undid my bun, too lazy and tired to wash my hair and dry it before bed. I turned off the bathroom light and opened the door to the hallway.

"Night!" Allison yelled out from the living room before I made it to my bedroom. "Sweet dreams, Sage."

I gazed down the dark hallway to where she sat, furrowing my eyebrows. She never said sweet dreams, but maybe she'd missed me too during all the months she'd had the apartment to herself. "You too, Al."

She giggled before shoving a handful of popcorn into her mouth, staring at me like I was something to be watched and not the movie playing on TV.

"Goofball," I whispered before turning the knob to my bedroom door. As soon as the door opened, I knew something was off.

There was a faint glow in the room. Candles? I pushed the door open farther, finally seeing my bed across the room, and it wasn't empty.

"Hey, darlin'. Miss me?" Austin asked with a smile, sitting on the edge of my bed in his uniform. God, he looked even better than I remembered.

"Oh my God!" I screeched and ran toward him, jumping into his arms before he had a chance to stand. "You're here. I didn't—"

He laughed, wrapping his arms around me tightly as I peppered his face in kisses. "I was a few hours late, but there was no way I was missing this day."

My belly flipped, and I pulled back, staring at the guy who'd worked his way into my heart. He was a cocky son of a bitch and could be annoying as hell, but he did it for me. "Aw. You must really like me," I teased, holding on to his neck like he was my lifeline or, if I let go, he'd somehow disappear.

His blue eyes sparkled in the dim lighting of the room. "Like you?"

I nodded, running my fingernails across the skin near his hairline.

"Sage…" he said softly, staring me right in the eyes.

My heart stopped. Was he going to say he loved me? Were we at that point in our relationship. I'd never said those words to anyone before except my family. And while I had strong feelings for Austin, stronger than I'd had for anyone else ever, I wasn't sure I was ready to say the words back to him.

"I wouldn't miss your homecoming for the world. I've waited seven long months for this night."

"To get laid."

"No, baby. To make love to you."

"Oh," I whispered, my belly doing that crazy flipping thing again.

He started to loosen his hold on me. "But maybe you don't want to."

I tightened mine. "No. No. I want. I want."

God, how I wanted him. I was hornier than I'd ever been in my life. Ship life wasn't conducive to masturbation, and there had been no one on board I'd wanted to mess around with. Even though Austin and I had never said we were exclusive, it still would've felt like I was cheating if I had.

He leaned in to kiss me, and I pulled back more, knowing what I needed to say before we went any further.

"What are you doing?"

"I have to say something."

He sighed. "Talk quick because my cock is telling me words aren't necessary."

I giggled, pressing my middle against his hardness. Yep. He was right. His dick didn't seem to care what I had to say, but I needed to express how I felt before we moved forward. "I missed you too," I said simply. "More than I ever thought possible."

He smirked, moving us toward the bed. "Is that it, or do you have a speech planned?"

"Asshole," I mumbled, but I didn't get another word out before his lips captured mine.

He fell backward onto my bed, me tumbling on top of him.

"I'd love to say I'm going to fuck you for hours, but in reality," he said as he undid the buttons on his shirt while I unbuckled his pants, "it's been seven months, and I'm pretty sure it's going to be quick."

"Can you do it more than once?" I asked, trying not to laugh my ass off because he was being honest.

His hands paused, and I smacked them because he was wasting time. "Can I fuck you more than once?"

I narrowed my eyes, yanking on his pants because I wanted to see him naked and I needed his cock inside me. "Yes, Austin, can you fuck more than once, or are you a one-and-done?"

His eyebrows furrowed. "There's a guy out there who's a one-and-done?"

"I don't know. I need answers. I want to know what I'm in for."

"You're in for being very, very tired tomorrow and not being able to walk right, darlin'," he said, shimmying out of his dress shirt before tossing it to the floor.

"I better fuckin' be, or we're going to have issues."

"Horny little tiger." He chuckled.

"Just make love to me and shut up," I told him.

"I love when you're bossy and full of sass."

"Then hold on, baby—" I reached inside his pants, fisting his cock as the head peeked out of the opening "—'cause I'm taking the reins."

"Even better," he mumbled as he undid my robe

and reached for my breast. "Fuckin' better than I ever imagined."

I shrugged the robe off my shoulders, letting it pool around my waist, fully exposing myself to him. "You have thirty seconds to get your pants off, or I'm starting without you."

He pushed me off him, and I fell to the side as Austin jumped from the bed, making quick work of any clothing left on his body.

I lay there staring at his naked body, something I'd never seen before…at least not his.

He was a work of art. All muscle and his cock…a masterpiece.

He dove onto the bed next to me, dick straight up in the air like a flagpole. "I'm ready for you to have your way with me. Do your damage."

I crawled on top of him, laying my body flat but careful not to impale myself on him. "First, we kiss."

He groaned, but as soon as my lips covered his, he stopped his whining and gave in. When his hands gripped my hips, I knew I was where I was always meant to be.

CHAPTER 16
AUSTIN

SAGE INTERLOCKED her fingers with mine as she rested her head on top of my shoulders. "How long are you here for?"

"Tomorrow." I squeezed her hand, hating that the trip couldn't be longer. "I tried for more, but I have to go out of the country for a bit."

She peered up at me, her eyes soft and sad. "Where are you going?"

"I can't say," I whispered, kissing her forehead where her fine lines had deepened from her sorrow.

Sage sighed as she looked away from me. "I figured, but it was worth a shot. Are you going into danger?"

"No," I lied. "It's just a fact-finding mission."

"Good."

She knew I was lying but didn't call me on it. She must have known every mission had an air of danger to it. She couldn't have been raised by a former SEAL and not know that was the case. But the last thing I wanted to do was add any bit of worry to her life right now. There was too much for a sailor to be happy about when they got their feet back on dry land.

"Will you spend the day with me…with us?"

I'd dreaded this moment. It was one thing to meet Sage's parents, even have breakfast with her dad, but to spend the day with them was something entirely different.

"Please," she begged. "I spent the day with your family."

She was right. She walked into my family's house, not knowing a single soul, and had no problem sliding right into the group. I needed to stop being such an asshole and suck it up. I could do a day with her parents and kid brother. I'd do anything to keep her happy this weekend. "Okay. I'll go."

Sage's entire demeanor changed in that split second. She rolled over, getting on all fours as she hovered over me. "You made me the happiest girl in the world."

I reached a hand up, grabbing the back of her neck. "You have low expectations, darlin'." I scanned her face, trying to memorize every feature. I needed the visual to keep me going on my next mission, giving me a reason not to do anything stupid and above the call of duty that'd put me in a body bag.

"I'm a realist, Austin. Not many boys want to spend time with my parents. They're a little much."

I pulled her face closer, our lips almost touching. "I'm not a boy, Sage, I'm a man."

She quirked an eyebrow as she stared down at me. "You sure?" she teased.

I moved quick, flipping our positions until she was pinned under me. "I proved it last night, baby."

Her face turned the lightest shade of pink as she bit the corner of her bottom lip.

"You need me to jog your memory?" I leaned forward, ready to taste her again.

But there was a knock on her bedroom door. "Sage…?" Allison, her roommate, called softly. "You in there?"

"Fuck," Sage groaned, closing her eyes. "It was just about to get good."

I rolled to the right, coming to a rest at her side. I grabbed a pillow from behind my head, placing it over my middle to cover up any evidence of what Allison had interrupted.

Sage smacked the pillow and laughed before she called out, "Come in."

The door opened at a painfully slow pace before Allison popped her head into the opening. "Shit." Her eyes widened as soon as they landed on me in the bed. "Did I interrupt something important?"

"Yes," I said.

"No," Sage said immediately afterward, giving the

pillow another smack in warning before she pulled herself into an upright position. "We were just talking."

"Liar," I muttered under my breath, covering the pillow with my arms before she had a chance to throw hands again.

"What's up?" Sage asked.

Allison opened the door wider and stepped into Sage's bedroom. "Well, there's a party on the beach tonight. I thought maybe you two would want to come with me."

In all honesty, I'd rather have my fingernails ripped out one by one than go to a beach party where people were going to act a fool. I'd spent most of my teenage years at things like that, and they always ended the same way—drunk and dumb.

Sage glanced at me like I was going to give an answer to that question.

"Whatever you want," I told her.

"What time are you leaving tomorrow?" she replied.

"Before sunrise."

Her lips turned down as she moved her gaze back to Allison. "We'll have to pass this time, but I'll go with you next time, Al."

Allison tucked a lock of her hair behind her ear as she nodded. "It's cool. I understand. If I had a man in my bed, I'd say no too. Hell, at this point, I'd take any warm body."

"I'm sure you'll find one tonight," I told her, knowing there would be a hookup at the beach… there always was.

Allison snarled. "The selection around here is atrocious, and I'd prefer not to get involved with a military man." Her eyes slid to mine. "No offense."

"None taken," I told her with a wink. "All men are shit, but military ones are the worst."

Sage turned her head to glare at me. "Does that include you?"

"I'm different," I promised her. But was I?

My track record was nothing to be proud of. I'd never been in a relationship longer than a few months, and even then, I'd never given a shit about making the woman happy. I was in it for myself, and I didn't take their feelings into consideration in the slightest, which was why I probably cheated more than I stayed faithful.

It wasn't like I'd had good role models growing up. My parents were like oil and water and did nothing to hide it from Pike and me either.

Sage rolled her eyes. "That remains to be determined."

I'd never been with someone as long as I'd been with Sage. But then again, we weren't really together, together. We'd spent more time apart than we had with each other. It was the perfect type of relationship for someone who disliked commitment. But I knew this couldn't last forever. At some point, we'd have to make a decision. But for now, the navy took that choice away from us.

"He probably has women all over the world," Allison said with a snort. "He's everywhere, always."

I glanced up at the ceiling, wishing the chick would shut her mouth. I liked Allison, but I didn't have women everywhere. But she planted that seed in Sage's mind, and now I'd have to pay for it.

"Do you?" Sage asked.

I glanced at her, taking in the seriousness of her expression. Her perfect pouty lips were flattened. "Do I what?" I replied, but I knew exactly what and why she asked.

"Have women everywhere?"

I sighed, pressing my fingers into the corners of my eyes. "No, Sage. I have one woman, and she's here. No one else. Nowhere else. Only the one. Only you."

Sage waved her hand in my direction. "Do you believe him?" she asked Allison and not me.

Allison nodded quickly. "I do. He flew here for you."

Sage grunted before she told Allison, "Men will do crazy things for good pussy."

I scoffed, hating that she didn't seem to understand. "I'm not flying across the country for a piece of ass, Sage. Jesus." I pushed myself up and off the bed.

But before I could get more than a step away, Sage clamped her hand around my wrist. "Wait."

I glanced at her over my shoulder, trying to bite back my temper. "What, Hill?"

She narrowed her gaze. "Oh, now it's Hill?"

I shrugged off her grip. "You're talking like it is."

"Don't go," she begged as her eyes softened. "I didn't mean it."

"Well, I think I've kicked the hornet's nest enough. I'm going to dip," Allison said, backing out of the bedroom quicker than she'd walked in.

"I know this is more," Sage said to me as she crawled off the bed and straightened her tank top where it had ridden up and exposed her stomach. She stepped in front of me, blocking the doorway. "Do you think I'd invite you to spend the day with my family if I thought we were just a casual thing?"

I blew out a breath, staring down into her green eyes. "I don't know, Sage. I don't know." I shook my head, wishing the entire conversation had gone a different way. "I want to believe it."

Sage wrapped her arms around my waist and hugged me. "It's more to me," she admitted. "And I know I'm more to you than a piece of ass."

My arms slid around her like they were always meant to be there. "There's nothing casual about the way I feel."

"Aww. You caught feelings for me?"

I laughed as I pressed my forehead to hers. "Something like that."

She moved her hand to my ass before she took a handful, giving it a hard squeeze. "I'd love nothing more than to stay in bed and explore those feelings today, but we have to meet my parents, and we're already cutting it close."

"I only need a shower. I can be ready in five."

"Fuckin' men," she muttered.

I pulled myself away and spun her around, giving her a little push before swatting her ass. "Get moving, sailor."

She lifted her arm, giving me the middle finger as she marched into the bathroom, and I quickly followed.

"So, Moore. What's your plan?" Sage's dad asked as we walked out of the restaurant.

"My plan, sir?" I asked, confused. "As in life, or…"

Her father stopped walking, and I slammed on the brakes, taking a few steps back. I looked ahead to where Sage, her mother, and brother were walking, oblivious that we were right behind them.

"What are your plans with my daughter?" he clarified as he stared at me.

I didn't answer right away, not wanting to fumble

through the answer. The last thing I needed was for her father to think I was a bigger idiot than he probably already did.

"I'm in this for the long haul, sir."

He raised an eyebrow, studying my face. "Sage acts tough, but she has a tender heart. I don't want her heart broken, Moore. If you're not in this for the right reasons, you should end it sooner than later."

"Again, I'm in this for the long haul, sir. I'm taking a risk being with her. I know I could get my ass into some trouble, but Sage is worth it."

"Do you want to get married?"

I swallowed, thinking about the question. "Someday."

"Soon?"

"I don't know… Eventually."

"Daddy," Sage said as she stalked our way, glaring at her father. "Stop it."

"It's okay," I told her, not wanting it to appear that I needed to be rescued from a conversation I'd figured her father and I would have eventually. "We're fine, darlin'."

"Darlin'?" her father muttered under his breath before he turned his attention to Sage. "We're just having a friendly chat."

I had to hold in my laughter at his statement.

She peered up at her father, looking like a little hellion. "It didn't sound friendly."

"It was, baby. It was." He smiled at her, and I thought for a minute she might believe him.

She rolled her eyes. "Why are you asking him if he wants to get married? Isn't that a question you should be asking me?"

He jerked his head back before shrugging. "It's something men talk about with their daughter's boyfriend."

"Patriarchal bullshit," Sage mumbled, straightening her shoulders. "Maybe I don't want to get married, and by you asking him that question, you're planting seeds for something that I maybe don't want to grow."

I stared at her, shocked. "You don't want to get married someday?"

"Shh," she said, holding up her hand in my face, shutting me down. I couldn't even be mad. She was too damn beautiful, and when she was pissed, she was fire.

He crossed his arms over his chest as he widened his stance. "Since when don't you want to get married? What the hell happened?"

"I never said that, Dad. I said maybe I don't, but even if I do, you should be asking me about my future plans and not Austin." She swung her gaze toward me and smiled. "Ignore him," she said as she pitched her finger toward her father. "He's being nosy and inappropriate."

I reached out and grabbed her hand. "Sage, we're fine. I promise. He wasn't being rude."

"Sage," her mother called out, motioning for her to come back to where she was standing. "I want you to see it." She pointed toward a shelf of trinkets outside a small bookshop.

"Fuck," Sage hissed. "Behave." Those words were meant for her father and not me.

He waited for her to walk away before he turned toward me in astonishment. "What got into her?"

I shrugged. "I don't know. She's a bit…"

"Don't say it. She might hear and go ballistic on you this time."

I laughed as I took a step forward, knowing hanging back would only end in a very pissed-off Sage. Not with me, though, but with her dad. "I'm not worried."

Her father walked next to me, keeping pace. "Sage said you have to leave tomorrow."

"I wish I could stay longer, but duty calls."

"Leaving the country?"

"Yeah, but you know how it is. I can't say to where."

He nodded. "I remember, and I don't miss those days."

"It wasn't an issue until now."

His eyes swung to me in full understanding. "Relationships make doing your duty harder. I've been there. And not being able to tell them where you are or what you're doing adds another layer."

"Completely. How did you handle it?"

"Well, Bobbie understood. She was off doing things she couldn't talk to me about either. I know Sage understands. She grew up in that life."

She understood, but that wouldn't make it easier on either of us. I also knew that someday, when I had my own kids, I didn't want them to live that kind of life.

"How long do you have left on your contract?"

"One year."

"You going to re-up?"

I shrugged one shoulder. "I haven't decided."

"Sage has a few years left."

"I know, sir. I'm aware."

"Long-distance isn't easy."

"Know that too." But being close hadn't been easy for me in the past either. Before Sage, I didn't think I could do something long-term and stay faithful.

"Daddy," Sage warned, eyeing us we got closer.

"We're not talking about you, sweetheart. We're talking about his contract."

Her eyes narrowed for a brief second before she went back to looking at bullshit with her mom.

We stood a few feet away and watched as they shopped. "When did you realize it was your time to get out?" I asked him.

He sighed, looking more relaxed than he had

before. "When it no longer became fun and the thought of leaving my wife and kids...maybe forever if a mission went south, became too much to bear."

I chewed on his words as I watched Sage.

I never thought much about the danger I often put myself into because I wouldn't be leaving anyone behind besides my brother and his family. But now, with Sage, I had someone else to think about.

And if this went further and longer than I'd ever imagined, I didn't think I could continue to risk my life, even if it was the only thing I'd ever known.

CHAPTER 17
SAGE

THERE WAS nothing like being in your own bed again after being away for months on end. I didn't think I'd ever slept so well in my entire life, even if I had to share the space with another human. But not just any person, a hunk of a man who basically threw flames off his skin in his sleep.

It was just after four in the morning. The moon was bright, streaming in between the curtains, much like the sun did near dusk.

"Morning," Austin whispered at my side before his eyes slowly opened.

I tucked my hand under my cheek, staring at him. "Morning."

He reached a hand out, placing it on my arm. "Sleep well?"

"Yes," I lied. The sleep I had gotten was great, but

it wasn't long-lasting like the night before. The knowledge that Austin was leaving and could be in harm's way weighed heavy on my mind.

I didn't know how my mom had handled it when my father was still a SEAL. Austin and I weren't even far into our relationship, but there was a pit deep in my stomach I couldn't quite shake.

"What's wrong?" he asked, his eyes searching my face as they tried to focus.

"Nothing."

He swept his thumb across the delicate skin of my forearm. "Are you worried?"

"Of course I am." I squeezed my eyes shut, wishing I didn't care as much as I did. If something happened to him…

"I'll be fine. I promise."

"You don't know that."

He scooted closer to me and pulled me tight against his chest. "I believe it. I don't go out into the field and think I won't come back."

I snuggled against him, listening to the slow, steady beat of his heart inside his solid, warm chest. "I've never felt this way…this heaviness."

"Aww," he whispered against my hair as he swept his fingers along my spine. "You really do have feelings for me."

"Now's not the time to joke," I grumbled against his skin as I sank into him as far as I could without entering his body.

"Darlin'," he said softly, pulling himself back. "Look at me."

"I don't want to," I said, being a brat and wallowing in my emotions.

"Please," he begged.

I tipped my head back, my green eyes meeting his.

"I promise I'll come back to you."

I was sure every SEAL who'd ever gone on a mission had whispered those same words to the woman they loved, and many of them didn't make it back.

"I won't do this forever."

"How long are you going to stay in?"

I had no right to ask in a moment like this. I'd known what I was getting into when things started with Austin. Maybe not at first since he didn't come right out and tell me he was part of one of the most elite fighting forces on the planet, but I knew soon enough and still didn't push him away.

"I have a year left on my contract and a lot of decisions to make between then and now."

My eyes burned at the thought of a year of this worry. "Which way are you leaning?" I couldn't stop myself from asking the question, but I wasn't sure I wanted the answer.

Austin's sigh said everything I needed to know. "I'm in the middle."

"And if I weren't around?"

"I'd stay in. There wouldn't be a reason to leave."

I let that simmer deep in my soul. I was important enough in his life that he'd leave the only thing he'd ever truly loved doing. I wasn't sure how I felt about that. I never wanted to be the type of woman who changed the very core of a man.

"Don't leave on my account. You love being a SEAL."

He pressed his lips against my hair again, holding me tighter. "I love being alive more than being a SEAL, Sage. Eventually, my luck would run out. I think I've spent enough time away from my family, running from whatever I thought I was missing and searching for."

"So, it's not only because of me?"

"No, but you're a big part."

"A lot can happen in a year," I say softly.

"Are you already planning on breaking up with me?" His body shook with laughter as he held me. "You're ridiculous sometimes."

"I have years left on my contract, Austin. I'm stuck doing whatever they tell me."

"Is this your final duty station?"

"It's supposed to be."

"Then you'd only be a short car ride away. I like that a hell of a lot more than all the way on the other side of the country. We'd figure it out."

"Yeah. I guess," I whispered against his skin.

"I have to go in a few minutes."

I closed my eyes again, wanting to stay in this moment forever. "It's so early."

"You can catch a few more hours of shut-eye."

"I'd sacrifice my sleep for more time."

He pulled back again, lifting my chin up with his two fingers until I was staring him straight in the eyes. "This isn't goodbye, Sage."

"I know, Austin."

"The only easy day was yesterday," he said before kissing my lips so softly, if I weren't looking, I wouldn't have known he did.

"But was it, though?"

Austin smiled and rubbed his nose against mine. "It was."

"My dad was being a pain in the ass."

"He was fine, darlin'. Nothing I couldn't handle."

Austin thought everyone was fine. After dealing with people in his military life and his time when he was younger, nothing much bothered him—even an overprotective father.

My father had years of experience in chasing guys out of my life. He was a professional at it, even. No one lasted longer than a few dates before they became too intimidated by his very presence.

"He and I aren't all that different," he added.

Great.

They said you often ended up with someone like your father, and goddamn it, I had. I'd hit the old copy-paste on the life keyboard, creating a damn near replica.

"Stop reminding me of that."

Austin didn't reply with words. He leaned forward, pressing his lips against mine harder than he had before. The kiss was slow and long, deep and passionate. It conveyed so many emotions without our saying a single word.

This was a goodbye. Not a forever one, but one, nonetheless. I felt in my very core that he was promising to come back to me, but sometimes, words weren't enough.

He rolled on top of me, never breaking the kiss, and pressed his weight against me. He surrounded me, filling my senses with his very being.

"I'll miss you," he murmured against my lips.

"I'll miss you too," I said, never having uttered those words to anyone else except my family. "Fair winds and following seas."

He hovered over me, the muscles on his arms defined and itching to be touched. "I'll text or call as soon as I'm able."

"I'll keep my phone with me at all times."

"It'll be a few days," he added so I wouldn't go out of my mind right away, but it didn't help. I'd start staring at the damn thing by later today, no matter what he said or what I told myself.

He pulled himself away from me, and I

immediately missed the heaviness of his weight and the warmth of his body. I propped myself up on my elbows, watching as he gathered his clothes off the floor.

The man was stunning. Not overly bulky, needing to keep himself flexible for some missions. But there wasn't an ounce of body fat on him. He wasn't bony either, but the perfect amount of mass to cuddle with.

The moonlight streamed, spotlighting where he stood, pulling on his jeans. "Are we okay?" he asked, staring at me with those haunting blue eyes.

"Why wouldn't we be?"

"That's not an answer."

"We're good…better than good."

He smiled easily as he yanked his wrinkled T-shirt over his head. "Good."

"Do you need a ride to the airport?"

He shook his head. "I'm getting picked up and flying out from base."

"Fancy," I mumbled.

"There are some perks to my rate."

"Guess so."

He stalked over to the side of the bed, leaning down to kiss me. He paused for a second, scanning my face. "Promise me you won't worry."

"I promise," I lied.

One corner of his mouth quirked up. "You're a shit liar, Hill."

"I try." I gave him the biggest, cheesiest smile. "I wasn't trained like you were."

"Thank fucking God for that."

"Keep my side of the bed free. I'll be back to fill it as soon as I can," he said before crashing his lips down on mine, stealing my breath.

My eyes stung again as my nose tickled. This was it. He was leaving. What if he never came back? Fuck. I couldn't do this shit forever. My heart couldn't take it, and neither could my mental health.

"I'll keep it warm for you," I said before he marched out of the room, leaving me behind.

———

"You okay?" Allison asked as we sat at the galley, eating a stale bagel and drinking watered-down coffee. Only the best for America's sailors.

"I'm fine."

"The redness in your eyes and dark bags underneath say otherwise."

"I slept like shit."

She raised a perfectly plucked eyebrow. "Did you cry?"

I shrugged. I had. I'd shed tears for a man who wasn't supposed to be anything to me. God, he had been so annoying the night I'd met him. I hadn't wanted to like him. I'd done everything I could to shut myself down from falling for him. When had the change happened? When had my feelings shifted? His family. Seeing him surrounded by them, watching the love flow both ways, made him damn near impossible not to like.

"He'll be back," she said to me as she smeared more brandless cream cheese on her overly toasted bagel. I swore the girl liked cream cheese more than she liked the bread. "He's tough."

"I know," I said, and while he was tough, that didn't mean he was immortal. Even the biggest, baddest person in the world couldn't outrun death.

"We should go out tonight."

I watched in horror as she used her finger to get the rest of the cream cheese out of the little plastic container and jammed it into her mouth. "I'm too tired for that. Rain check?"

She nodded, practically moaning as she savored the cream cheese. "Hell yeah. I could use a night out, but I'll need time to plan my outfit."

Besides cream cheese, Allison also had an unhealthy obsession with fashion. When she wasn't in her pajamas or uniform, she was dressed to kill and spent almost her entire check every month buying only the best. But she wasn't like that until I got back from deployment. It's like a switch got flipped while I was gone.

"Will Austin be okay with you going out?"

I jerked back my head at her question. "Why wouldn't he be?"

She shrugged as she lifted the bagel to her lips, staring at it like it held all the secrets to the universe. "I don't know. My last boyfriend, Ezra, he forbade me to go out."

"What?" I widened my eyes at the stupidity. A man like that deserved to be kicked straight in the nuts and told to go to hell. "That's the dumbest shit I've ever heard. I hope you told him to go fuck himself."

She gave me a cream-cheese smile. "It's why he's my ex," she said with a chuckle. "Fuck that, and fuck him too."

"I wouldn't put up with that, and Austin doesn't seem to be the type. He hasn't tried anything like that yet."

Allison licked her fingers near the edge of the bagel, getting every last drop of cream cheese. She was starting to get an audience from the men around us. No doubt they were picturing her relishing their cocks the same way she was making love to the bagel. "Men suck sometimes."

"You think?" I said, unable to stop my chuckle. "If you don't stop it, you're going to give every man in this room wood."

Her eyes moved around the Galley, finally realizing she was being watched. "Fuck them. Let them suffer."

I nodded my agreement. Most of the men in this room were indeed pigs. They treated women like dirt and thought of them as nothing more than a means to an end.

"I love when you're rotten, Al."

She set down her bagel, licking each one of her fingers as slowly as possible, even the ones without any cream cheese. "Men are too easy."

"They're led around by their dicks."

She nodded as she took her thumb deep, making more than a few grown men groan their frustration. "This is way too easy."

"Stop being a tease."

"A girl's gotta eat."

"Not like she's going hard on a dick, babe."

She giggled as she finally decided to use the tissue paper-like napkin I'd pushed her way when we'd first sat down. "That's why we have to go out. I need to get laid—and not by a navy man either. If I go much longer, one of these douchebags is going to end up inside me."

I grimaced. "That would be criminal."

"Completely uncalled for and unnecessary. There're too many yummy men out there in the world to limit myself to such mediocre options."

"We'll get you laid," I promised her.

"After listening to you two going at it all weekend, I need some cock before I combust."

My face heated as I wiped my lips, trying to hide my horror at the knowledge that she'd overheard us fucking. "I'm sorry," I mumbled into the napkin.

She waved her freshly licked fingers in the air. "Don't be. It was better than watching porn."

I didn't know if I should be proud or horrified that she'd pleasured herself to our noises.

"Was it as hot as it sounded?" she asked.

"Hotter," I told her with a wink.

CHAPTER 18
AUSTIN

"THIS IS MY LAST," Maverick said as he did an ammo check of his weapon.

"Wait, what?" Wiz asked, leaning forward like he didn't quite hear him right.

"I put in my paperwork. I'm out after this."

There was a stunned silence in the back of the plane as all three of us let those words sink in.

"I can't fuckin' believe it." Trigger shook his head as he ground his teeth together in disappointment. "She finally got to you."

"Be happy for me," Mav added, knowing the news wouldn't land well. "She's pregnant, and I don't want to leave my wife and kid behind because I had to scratch some macho itch and childhood superhero fantasy. I'm getting too old for this shit. I'm in my thirties, for Christ's sake."

His words struck like a bag of bricks slamming into my chest.

"Fuck, man. Congrats on the kid," Wiz said, trying to hide his unhappiness over the news. "I know you two have been trying for a while."

That was news to me. Maybe I'd been too wrapped up in whatever Sage and I had going on that I hadn't paid enough attention to what was happening with my closest friends.

"You'll be a great dad," I told him, happy as hell that he was going to get to move on to something bigger and better without ending up with his ass dead and buried in a hole somewhere. "You deserve this."

"You might not be far behind me," he replied as he continued to check his equipment.

We all did the same. Dropping news like that before a mission would've normally been a no-go, but we'd formed such a tight-knit group, this was old hat to us now.

The mission was supposed to be simple. We were extracting someone with limited security around them. An in-and-out job, something we wished every mission would be, but they never were.

"We're five out," Trigger announced, stashing a handful of things under his seat. "We have ten minutes to find the target, obtain him, and be at the rendezvous point for extraction."

We had nothing more to say to one another. This time was for final preparation. Everything that was said before had to be pushed out of our minds. Any distraction could lead to one of us coming out of here in a body bag. We had no room for error.

This was a job. One that I had no problem performing because it was only me I had to worry about. But Maverick had Lyndsey and now a baby on the way. He couldn't continue to put his ass in harm's way when he had them to worry about.

And now, I had Sage. I wasn't alone anymore. I knew this wasn't a lifetime gig. You either retired young or died before your time. Those were the only two options for a navy SEAL. This wasn't a long-term career. Every year, I could feel my body changing, no longer as strong or agile as the year before. My time was coming, but I wanted to have a reason to leave… someone to go for.

I pulled out the map, letting myself get lost in the details of what we were about to do. I pushed away thoughts of Maverick leaving, of Sage at home, of everything but the men in front of me and how to get us all out of here in one piece.

Five minutes later, right on cue, we had boots on the ground. Using our night vision, we navigated the terrain outside the compound, guns drawn, ready for anything and everything that would be thrown our way.

No matter how much we planned, there was always shit that would happen that we didn't account for. Luckily, we always had one another's backs. And honestly, we were fucking good at what we did.

Trigger pointed to the other side of the compound, giving us the sign to peel away from the group. My heart raced in my chest. The adrenaline spike was inevitable.

No matter how hard I tried to keep my ass cool, calm, and collected, the heat of the moment and the danger of the situation always seemed to creep in. It was what kept me alive and on my toes.

I hustled to my location without laying eyes on another soul, including the people who were supposed to be here guarding the target.

Something was off. Where were the people?

We'd had eyes on them not more than an hour ago, and they'd been here. We'd had visuals on five men outside the compound and no fewer than three others inside.

I turned the corner, ready to enter through the back, when there was a whistle, followed by my body being thrown backward, slamming into the sand.

Before I could do anything, my vision blurred, and the bright stars overhead turned black.

CHAPTER 19
SAGE

"MORNING, DAD."

"Hey, sweetheart. What are you doing?"

I leaned forward, staring at my reflection in the mirror as I smoothed down a stray hair. "Getting ready for work. You?"

"Same. Same," he said, but there was something in his voice that made me glance down at the phone screen, waiting for him to drop some news.

"What's up, Dad? You don't usually call this early."

My dad was nothing if not predictable. He called on weekends, and when he didn't, it was because he had something important he needed to tell me. It wasn't the weekend.

"Don't panic."

My stomach immediately sank. Nothing good ever started with those two words. "What happened?"

"I want you to know he's in serious but stable condition."

My body went backward until my ass hit the wall, and I used it to keep me upright. "Did Sawyer get into a car accident?" My breathing picked up as my heart hammered faster.

Serious but stable still meant he was in bad shape…that was what the serious part indicated.

"No, baby. Not Sawyer."

I blinked as I stared at my reflection, but I seemed so far away, as if I was in a tunnel. "What? Who?"

"Austin," my father breathed.

My knees wobbled as my ass slid down the wall until I landed on the floor. "How bad?" I whispered, feeling my eyes start to burn.

"He was shot a few times and is pretty beat-up."

"He was shot a few times?" I repeated his words, trying to make them sink in, but my brain couldn't seem to accept what had happened as real. "Are you sure?"

"Baby," Dad whispered back. "I'm sure."

"When?"

"Two days ago, on his mission."

"Where?"

"I don't know where they were."

"No, Dad. Where was he shot?"

Every small sound in the building seemed to disappear, and all I could hear was my breathing, my father's voice, and the beating of my own heart.

"The leg, shoulder, and upper thigh."

"Fuck. That's insane."

"I know, Sage. That's a lot of holes, but he's safe now and getting the medical help he needs."

"Which hospital?" I had the urge to run out the door and head in whatever direction he was in, even if I knew it was impossible. That was how it worked in the military. Your life was not your own, even for boyfriends who were filled with bullet holes.

"He's in Germany right now, but he'll be back in the States as soon as he's stable enough for transport."

"Damn," I muttered, squeezing my eyes shut. My chest hurt, the ache so deep I doubled over, nearly touching my forehead to the cold tile of the bathroom floor. "I want to see him."

"I'll pull some strings and see what I can do. Don't hold your breath, though. I'll make sure he gets a phone, so you can at least talk to him."

"Thanks, Dad."

His voice would have to do. It was better than nothing, and at least I'd know he was still breathing.

"You promise he's okay?"

Dad sighed, heavy and loud. "He's in serious condition, but he's stable, baby. He's a strong guy. I'm sure he'll pull through."

Strength didn't mean he was invincible. There wasn't a person on this planet who could outrun death, no matter how many muscles he had, including Austin.

"Keep your phone nearby. I'll update you as soon as I hear more."

"I will."

"Talk soon, baby."

"Dad," I called out before he had a chance to disconnect. "How did you find out?"

My father wasn't in the military anymore, but he still had friends who were part of the SEALs. It was a brotherhood that time, distance, and age didn't seem to tear apart.

"James called me after the navy contacted Pike. He wanted to make sure you knew what was going on."

Shit. Pike had to be beside himself. Austin was the last of his family, and I knew how important the two of them were to each other, even if they didn't see each other often. Men were weird like that.

"Pike has to be a wreck."

"Pike's in contact with the hospital, and James will let me know when he knows more. I'm going to run and make some calls about Austin. See what else I can find out."

Dad did have a lot of connections in the navy. Always had and still did to this day. Once a sailor, always a sailor.

"As soon as I get information, I'll send it your way. I promise."

"Thanks, Dad."

"Love you, kiddo."

"Love you too," I said before he ended the call.

I stared at the beat-up wood on the cabinet under the sink, still in shock over what my father had just said.

Austin had been shot.

Not just shot, but shot three times.

He was in serious condition but was stable.

He wasn't in the country and not even on the same continent as me.

I had no way to get to him because in the eyes of the military, he wasn't direct kin or a spouse. Therefore, I couldn't even ask for leave to be with him.

The only thing I could do now, besides having a panic attack, was to go to my commanding officer and beg to use my leave for a few days so I could get eyes on Austin and make sure for myself that he was still breathing and going to be okay.

I brushed away the few tears that had trickled down my cheeks and took a couple deep, calming breaths. He was okay. He was going to stay okay. He would live.

I reminded myself of those things as I pushed myself up and off the floor, dusting off my uniform so I wouldn't get in trouble once my ass hit the gate.

Since my ship was in dry dock, getting more repairs, I'd been helping out and doing another rate that wasn't my own. I'd been working at the gate, checking IDs, and questioning base visitors for a few days. And when I said it was mind-numbing…it was mind-numbing.

"You want a ride today?" Allison asked before I had a chance to take two steps out of the bathroom.

"Yeah," I said, but my voice quivered.

Allison looked up, her eyes going wide when she saw the tear marks I didn't wipe away very well from my cheeks. "What happened?" she asked as she rushed over to me, touching my arm. "Who do I need to murder?"

"It's Austin."

"I'll hurt that man if he so much—"

"He got shot," I blurted out before she had a chance to finish that statement.

"Oh my God," she gasped, her hand tightening on my arm.

"He was shot three times, actually. He was shot three times," I babbled, unable to stop myself from saying the words, even though they still didn't feel real.

"That's fucking bananas."

"I know." I sniffled as the tears threatened to fall again. "He's in Germany, and I don't know anything other than he's serious but stable."

Allison immediately pulled me into an embrace and rubbed my back. "He'll be okay," she promised. "He's too tough to die."

That was always the line and the lie, but for right now, I'd let myself believe it. I placed my head on her shoulder, soaking in the little bit of comfort I could get in this moment.

"Can we go see him?"

"No," I told her. "He's overseas still."

"Fuck. That sucks."

"Tell me about it," I mumbled against her T-shirt.

Allison didn't have to work today, but she was going to head to the Nex for some groceries and a few items for the apartment. If she were in uniform, she wouldn't let me be a blubbering mess on the pristine material.

"Come on, chick. I'll drive you in, and if you need anything—I mean anything—I'll come back and grab you. I'm not going anywhere today."

I pulled away from her embrace, trying to make myself presentable. The last thing I wanted was for anyone to see me with bright red eyes and tear-stained cheeks.

"You think this will go away before we get there?" I asked, waving my hand in front of my face.

She sucked in air between her teeth. "Maybe."

"Liar," I muttered.

"You know men. They're clueless and don't pay attention to much, especially when it comes to anything that has to do with feelings and emotions."

I cracked a smile. "That ain't no lie, Al."

"I learned that hard lesson a long time ago." She threw her arm around my shoulder, moving me to the counter where my bag sat. "We better run before you're late. You don't want to get your ass chewed out."

I grabbed my bag and slung it around my shoulder as soon as Allison dropped her arm. "I don't think I could deal with that today."

She shook her head. "You'd probably pop off and end up in shit so deep, even your daddy couldn't get you out of it."

"Yep, and that's not what I need right now."

"Nope, but tonight, you're going to need some wine." She smiled at me as we walked out the front door. "Scratch that. You're going to need a lot of wine."

"Tequila," I corrected her. "Until my face goes numb."

"So, one drink, then?" She bumped my arm with her shoulder. "You know you're a lightweight when it comes to your booze."

"I don't want to be drunk tomorrow, but I want to be oblivious tonight."

"I can make that happen," she said as we walked to her car and then headed toward the base.

CHAPTER 20
SAGE

MY PHONE VIBRATED in my pocket as soon as my boots hit the doorway to my apartment. I nearly jumped out of my skin after having been on edge the entire day.

My dad had called earlier, letting me know that not much had changed with Austin's condition and they were still assessing his wounds.

I hated waiting. I'd had shit patience since the day I was born. And being so far away, not being able to see for myself, was torture.

"Hello," I said, not recognizing the number.

"Sage?" a man's voice asked on the other end.

"Yes."

"It's Pike."

My body immediately locked up, overtaken by fear. His voice wasn't upbeat but stressed.

"Is he okay?" I asked, skipping the normal niceties people exchanged when they started a conversation.

Pike blew out a breath. "He's alive."

While that was great, that didn't give me a lot of information and definitely didn't give me the warm and fuzzies.

"Is he still in serious condition?"

"Yeah, darlin'."

Goose bumps spread across my skin when he used that term in the same manner as his brother. It had the same sweet undertone that made my heart flutter.

"But he's stable enough for them to do surgery to repair some of the damage. We'll know more once they get in there and see how bad the injuries are."

"Fuck," I muttered, toeing off my boots and kicking them to the side. "Is he strong enough for that?"

"The docs say he is, but who knows. I haven't been able to talk to him because they have him so doped up, he's knocked clean out and unable to talk."

"Shit. I was hoping to hear his voice."

"I know. I'm sure as soon as he's awake, he'll be screaming at them to bring him a phone because he'll want to talk to you too."

"You should talk to him first."

"Babe," Pike said, and I could tell he was about to lay down his thoughts about my statement. "He'll *want* to talk to you first, and I'm okay with that. You're his girl. I'd want to hear Gigi's voice first if I made it out of some shit like that alive. I wouldn't want to hear his scratchy deep voice until I'd had time to let my girl know I was alive and coming back to her."

Even in my panicked state, I swooned a little bit over Austin's brother. Gigi was a lucky woman, and I knew where Austin had learned how to treat a woman and how to love. Pike was a good teacher, and based on his answer, I was just as lucky as Gigi—or at least I would be in the future.

"Okay," I whispered as I sat down on the edge of the couch, too worried to get too comfortable.

I felt guilty going on and enjoying life while Austin was full of bullet holes, bleeding somewhere halfway across the world.

"The doctor said that if all goes well, he should be able to communicate about twenty-four hours after the surgery."

"If," I whispered to myself and away from the phone so Pike couldn't hear. My stomach knotted and everything that I had eaten today, which wasn't much because I'd been too nervous, threatened to make its way out of my body. "When's the surgery?"

"First thing tomorrow morning, but they're six hours ahead there, so he'll be a few hours in by the time you get up."

"Will you keep me updated? Send me a text or whatever, Pike. I don't want to be a bother, but I've been so worried sick, I don't think I'll be able to sleep tonight."

"He'd want you to get some rest. Don't worry yourself about things you can't control." He sounded so wise and older when he spoke.

"Are you going to sleep?"

He let out a little chuckle. "Fuck no."

"Babe, is that Sage?" Gigi asked in the background.

"Yep."

"Gimme the phone. I want to talk to her."

"Here," he said, and I heard some static and shuffling.

"Sage?" Gigi asked, her voice soft and gentle. "Are you okay?"

I let myself collapse backward. "I don't know."

"Honestly, me either," she admitted. "But he's tough, and I know he's doing everything in his power to get himself back to you."

"I know," I whispered, trying to will myself not to cry. With Pike on the line, I'd done my best to stay strong. Men tended to get weirded out by female emotion, but with Gigi, it was an entirely different energy.

"Do you need me to come be with you?" she asked, being so damn sweet.

Although it sounded nice, it was the last thing I needed or could handle. I had just enough energy to do my job. I didn't want to have to entertain someone else in my space. Allison would probably lose her mind too, even though she and Gigi would hit it off.

"No. I'm okay. I have to work all week, but as soon as I know he's going to be transferred, I'm going to beg and plead to get a few days off."

"Pike's going to see if he can be transferred to a hospital here in Florida once he heads back to the States."

My heart jumped at that news. "That would be great."

"Right?"

"Yeah," I mumbled, hopeful that he'd make it back to me.

"We can't travel too far with the kids and the business, but we want to be able to see him and help him in his recovery. We'll get it figured out. One step at a time."

First step was that he needed to make it out of surgery alive. "Make sure to let me know what's happening as soon as you know anything. Please."

"Of course, sweet pea. I'll add you into the group text we started. It's easier with so many people wanting updates. Is that okay?"

"That's perfect," I told her.

"Now, go take a nice hot bath and get some rest. Tomorrow's probably going to be stressful."

"And today wasn't?" I said sarcastically.

She laughed. "It was, but tomorrow will be worse."

"Fuckin' great."

"But I'm telling you now, he's coming home. I

never saw him as crazy about anyone as he is over you. He called me before he left for the mission and talked my ear off about everything. He's not leaving that behind."

I smiled to myself, the tears forming just as rapidly. "Thanks, Gigi."

"Who knows," she said quickly, "we could be sisters someday."

I was suddenly stunned into silence.

"Darlin', don't give the woman a panic attack. Jesus," Pike muttered in the background.

"She's not panicking," Gigi told him. "Are you, Sage?"

"No," I lied, somehow hiding the quaver in my voice. "I'm good."

"See," she said to Pike. "She's fine."

"Austin's going to be pissed when he wakes up and hears that you told her that."

"Who's going to tell him?" she said back to him with an edge to her voice.

"You. Her. Me."

"Babe, Sage, you tellin' him?"

"Um, fuck no." I shook my head to myself.

"Me either," she said. "You talkin' then, big man?"

"No fucking way."

"Then there's nothing to worry about," she told him.

"Mommy!" a high-pitched voice yelled in the background. "I need you."

"I got to run, Sage."

"Text me."

"On it," she said, and a second later, I had a message from the group text.

"Bye, guys," I said to them.

"Bye," they replied in unison before the call ended.

Gigi: I added Sage to the chat.

Me: Hi. Thanks, Gigi.

I swiped to the list of contacts, not recognizing a single number.

Unknown: Hey, sugar. How are you holding up?

Pike: Everyone send her your contact info so she isn't guessing who's who.

Within sixty seconds, each number sent me their contact information, and I added them to my phone nearly as quickly as they rolled in.

I could see then that Tamara had been the person to ask me the question.

Me: I'm doing as well as I can be in a situation like this.

Carmello: I guess I can't tease him about being a bulletproof superhero who's not as cool as Superman or Batman anymore.

Rebel: No, dumbass. You'll have to use a different annoying saying from now on.

I laughed a little at their banter, even if it was a bit dark. I'd spent the day freaking out almost alone, except for Allison and my dad, while they had each other. They were beyond lucky.

Carmello: Rocco, get your woman under control. She's being mean to me.

Rocco: Bro, sometimes you deserve it.

Arlo: Only sometimes?

Rocco: Does my brother have you "under control," Ar?

Arlo: LOL LOL LOL No. He likes to talk like he's in charge, but we know who holds the power.

Tamara: Pussy power, baby.

"Hey," Allison said as she walked into the living room, but I was too busy to notice with my face buried in my phone.

I glanced up, giving her a weak smile. "Hey."

"Any news?" She came over to the couch and sat down next to me, placing a glass of iced tea on the side table.

"He's having surgery tomorrow before they can move him."

"That's good, right?"

I shrugged a shoulder. "I think so. He's at least strong enough for surgery."

"He'll be okay," she replied, placing her hand on my arm and giving it a quick squeeze.

"His brother called, and now I'm in a group text with them. I should get updates quicker now."

"Is that what you were reading? Their texts?" She leaned over, trying to see my phone screen.

"Yeah. They're wild, but some of the most fun

and loving people I've ever met. And there're so many of them. It would make you dizzy."

"I love that they added you to the text. That's a pretty big step."

"Is it?" I gawked at her before my eyes flickered to my screen. "They just want me to know what's going on."

"His brother could've just texted you separately."

"He's trying to save time."

"Uh-huh," she muttered and then smiled. "Sure, babe. Whatever you need to tell yourself right now. You'll see."

"Only if he makes it, Al."

"He'll make it. I know these things."

"You're a psychic now?"

"I do have skills."

"I thought your skills were more about gobbling cock than knowing the future," I teased.

"I'm a woman of many talents." She laughed, smacking my leg. "Now, get your ass in the shower. You smell like salt water and sweat, and the combo isn't doing you any favors."

I sighed, feeling the exhaustion everywhere in my body. "I'm going. I'm going. Want a pizza? I'm starving."

"I'll order one while you're in there, and we can veg out on the couch until you pass out."

"Sleep isn't going to be easy tonight." I pushed

myself off the couch, and my feet instantly hurt as they landed on the hard floor.

"Mr. Tequila says otherwise," she said with a wink.

"You're the best kind of friend," I told her before I walked away.

"I got your back, babe. Now, go." She shooed me away from the couch. "We have a show to binge."

I did my best to smile and seem excited, but I knew I wouldn't be good company. My mind was elsewhere and would be until I saw him with my own eyes.

I COULDN'T STAND up straight as I walked the halls of the hospital, heading toward Austin's room. He'd made it out of surgery without any issues and had been transferred to a hospital near Gainesville two days later. As soon as I'd gotten the call, I'd hauled ass to get there. Luckily, it coincided with a few days I didn't have to be at work, and I didn't have watch.

As soon as I rounded the corner near the nurses station, I came to a screeching halt. I was expecting to see Pike and Gigi, and they were there, but they were also surrounded by the rest of the family.

Pike's head came up, his eyes landing on me. "Sage," he said as he let go of Gigi and stalked my way.

I swallowed, expecting to hear bad news. Why were they all here? Had things turned south within the last five hours it had taken me to drive there? "Hi," I squeaked out, unable to hide my nervousness.

Gigi walked behind him, giving me a small smile. I soaked that in and tried to shake off my jitters. "Hey, doll," she said.

"He's okay," Pike said, maybe reading my body language or the fact that I couldn't muster much of a smile when I saw them all. "He's asleep right now, but that's because they gave him some pain meds. He should be up soon."

"Did you talk to him?" I asked him, squeezing my hands at my sides as I tried to alleviate some of the panic that had built inside me since I'd heard he'd been wounded.

Pike nodded. "Yeah. He's still his same asshole self."

Gigi laughed. "Stop it. Your brother is a sweetie."

Pike rolled his eyes as he slid an arm over Gigi's shoulders. "He's an asshole too."

"Not to me," she argued.

"That's because you have boobs."

Gigi leaned her head against his shoulder and placed a hand on his stomach. "It's because I'm nice to him. You should try it sometime, grumpy."

"Anyway," Pike said, ignoring his wife's statement, "I spoke with the doctors a bit ago. He has some new hardware in him. A few steel rods and screws to keep shit together that had been shattered."

I winced. None of that sounded good, but he said

it like he was talking about the weather tomorrow. Men.

"They're going to get him up and walking sometime today. They don't want him lying around too long. It's not good for the body."

"Already?" I ask, shocked that someone could even stand after having rods and screws newly installed in their body.

Pike nodded. "It's crazy shit. They said with his physical shape, he shouldn't have any issues, but the therapy will still be tough. They expect him to make a full recovery."

I breathed a sigh of relief, but then one word in the last sentence repeated in my head. "They *expect* him to make a full recovery?"

"They can't give definites. You know how doctors are. All vague shit because they don't want to get their asses sued. He's going to be grumpy."

"Aww. You're going to be twinsies," Gigi added with a whoop of laughter. "The grump brothers."

I finally let myself relax a little. He was okay. He was stable. He was going to be getting out of bed. That was a good step in the right direction. Just knowing that he'd been transferred had been a relief. They wouldn't have done that if he were on his deathbed.

"Sage," Tamara called out, motioning me over to the rest of the group.

Gigi slid out from under Pike's arm and grabbed

my hand, pulling me toward the others. "Come on. Everyone's excited to see you."

They'd texted for hours upon hours over the last few days. They were great at keeping me informed and my mind off what had happened to Austin. I'd never met a funnier group of people, and the love they had for one another was unmatched.

From a distance, they looked like a ragtag group of people. From tattooed bikers to the bookworm type. Nothing about them as a whole made sense from the outside.

I should've been more settled in that moment, but I wasn't. With everyone here and knowing Austin was so close by, my body was filled with so many emotions.

"Hey, sweetie," Lily, Gigi's cousin, said to me as soon as I came within arm's reach. She didn't hesitate in pulling me into a tight embrace, something I didn't know I needed, but I did.

As soon as her arms were around me, my knees wobbled, and I had to do everything in my power to hold back my sob.

"He's okay," she whispered in my ear. "I promise."

"Thank you," I said, holding on to her like she was my lifeline in the moment. "I was so worried."

"We all were, Sage. When you love someone, it's natural to be so worried."

It hit me then. When I'd gotten off the ship, I couldn't say the words. I'd felt them, but I wasn't ready. If Austin had died on his mission, I never would've been able to say them to him. But I'd gotten a second chance, and I wouldn't squander the time now.

I did love him. I couldn't deny it or lie to myself anymore about how I felt. Although it was scary as hell to say those words to him, they needed to be said. I hoped he felt the same and said them back, but anything was possible, especially after a near-death experience.

"I need a hug too," Tamara said, pulling me out of Lily's arms. "You can't hog her."

I giggled a little, the heaviness of Lily's statement fading into the back of my mind a bit. "There's enough of me to go around."

Tamara's hug was rougher than Lily's, but that wasn't much of a surprise. I could picture Lily sitting at high tea with her pinkie held up in the air and fitting in perfectly. Tamara was a bit edgier, but no less sweet.

"Are you holding up okay?" she asked as she hugged me.

"I am, thanks to you guys," I admitted.

If it weren't for their text messages, I would've gone out of my mind with worry the last few days. They'd been my lifeline to sanity in this chaotic and stressful time.

Tamara let go of me, but her hands slid to my elbows and stopped. "That's what family is for, baby. You're one of us now."

My belly flipped. I wanted those words to be true. Even though I loved Austin, I wanted to be a part of this...of his family. "I don't know about that."

She squeezed my arms. "Trust me. You are. Once you're in, there's no getting out."

"Stop scaring her," Rebel said, moving me out of Tamara's grip. "You make us sound a little wacko."

"We *are* a little wacko, Reb. The sooner she understands and accepts that and us, even with our issues, the better."

I laughed. "You guys are great, and I don't like normal. Normal is boring."

Tamara waved her hand at me, staring at Rebel. "See? Perfect."

I smiled, shaking my head. "He's awake," Rocco said, peering into Austin's room.

"Let Sage go in first and alone," Pike commanded.

I rocked backward, surprised by his statement. "It's okay."

Pike shook his head. "Trust me, my brother wants to see you and no one else. We've all seen him already anyway. He wants you. He's been asking for you. Even the doctor on the phone before surgery said that he was calling out your name in and out of consciousness."

My chest ached at that statement.

"Go," Pike said, pushing me toward the doorway to Austin's room. "Take your time."

"We'll be here waiting," Tamara added.

"I'll make sure they don't eavesdrop," Gigi promised as I walked by her.

I stopped at the entrance to his room, glancing in. I took a moment to draw in a deep breath, preparing myself for whatever I saw inside. No matter what, I'd keep a smile on my face and stay positive. The last thing Austin needed was a woman crying over him while he was trying to recover or half out of it.

I let my gaze wander to his face, but his eyes were closed, and he looked so peaceful. I stepped inside, walking as softly as I could to not wake him up with the clicking of my shoes against the old linoleum floor.

So many emotions welled up inside me as I got closer, itching to touch him. I wanted to rush to his bed and curl up against him, feeling the warmth of his body for my soul to understand he was still alive. But I stopped myself, wanting him to get as much rest as possible so he could get out of here.

I sat in the chair next to him, unable to take my eyes off his face, ignoring the metal that surrounded his leg. His chest was bare except for a bandage around his shoulder, and it took everything in me not to reach out and place my hand over his heart to feel the steady beat.

"Sage," he whispered so softly, I barely heard him.

My gaze flickered to his face, and I was suddenly

overcome with relief. "Austin," I croaked out, my eyes instantly watering.

Shit. Way to be chill, Sage. I turned into a blubbering mess in under three seconds at the mere sound of my name.

He reached out an arm, holding out his hand. "I'm okay," he said, his eyes staring at me with such softness. "Don't cry, baby."

Those words only made me cry harder. I slid my hand into his, relishing the warmth of his skin against mine. He was fine. He was alive.

"I'm sorry." I sniffled, trying to push back the tears, but I failed. "I was so worried."

"Come closer." He gently yanked on my hand. "I need you near me."

"I don't want to hurt you."

"Darlin'…" He moved and winced for a second. "I can't be any more hurt than I already am."

I sniffled again, feeling a fresh set of tears ready to fall.

"Come on." He gave my hand another yank, and my feet came unstuck from the floor. "Sit next to me."

I stared down at the bed, trying to make sense of the tubes, cords, and everything else. Where would I sit that wouldn't hurt him?

As if reading my mind, he released my hand and pushed everything out of the way, lifting his paper-thin blanket and making room for me. "Here," he said as he glanced down at the empty spot.

"Austin." I didn't think it was a good idea. I was a clumsy person, and this could only end badly for him.

"I *need* you to be near me," he begged, coaxing me forward.

I moved slowly, placing my butt on the bed first and sitting like I was on top of a thin pane of glass. "Better?"

"No. Come closer." He snaked his arm around my waist, pulling me toward him.

For a man who had been near death and had three new holes in his body, he was still ridiculously strong. "I don't think the doctors will approve."

"Who cares what they say."

"You have to listen to them," I told him, letting myself relax a little against him to make him happy.

"I do, but they don't know everything I need to recover, and that includes having my woman next to me. Now, lie down."

He was so demanding, but I couldn't argue with him. He needed me, and I would do everything in my power to keep him happy.

I did as he told me, lying down next to him, but I was careful with my limbs. In my mind, he was still breakable.

"Snuggle in."

I stared up at him, wondering who this snuggle monster was. Austin was always sweet, but I figured he cuddled out of duty and not necessity. "I might hurt you."

He barked out a laugh, a sound that was so sweet it made my heart swell. "Hush up." He curled his arm around me, holding me close to his side. "This is just what I need. I wasn't sure I was going to get to do this again."

My stomach flipped as I stared up at him. "I was so scared."

"Me too, darlin'. Me too. When I woke up in the hospital, my body filled with pain, I knew there was a chance I wouldn't make it back to you."

I sagged against him, finally placing my hand on top of his chest to feel his heart. I was thankful I had a second chance with him. He could've been taken from me in the blink of an eye, and I didn't want the opportunity to pass me by again. "I love you, Austin," I blurted out, unable to hold it in anymore.

A slow, sweet smile spread across his face. "Darlin'," he whispered.

My stomach sank when he didn't say it back right away. I was starting to panic, thinking the feelings weren't mutual.

"I love you too, Sage. I realized the moment I was shot that there was no place I'd rather be than with you."

I let his words wash over me. The feelings weren't one-sided. Neither of us had rushed into this. This was real. We were real.

"It's too bad we're going to be stuck in different places for a while."

"Not for long," he replied and kissed the top of my head. "Broken SEALs aren't of much use to the navy. I'll be getting a medical discharge, probably before my ass even has a chance to get comfy back in my apartment in California."

I peered up at him, both sad and happy. "You think so?"

He nodded and blew out a breath. "It was time anyway. Even if three bullets hadn't taken away my career, it was going to be time to retire. As soon as they let me out, I'll come to you."

"You're going to move to Pensacola?" I gaped at him.

Not that Pensacola was bad, but it sure as hell wasn't nice either. Most navy towns were crap. Although the water was nearby, it didn't have much else going for it.

"You're there, so that's where I'm going to be. We spent enough time apart. I figure it's about damn time we figure out where this is going. But whatever happens, I want to be where you are."

"Wow," I breathed.

"Unless you don't want me there."

"No. No. I want you close to me. After this—" I waved my free arm toward his steel-caged leg "—I don't want to spend any more time apart. And I'd be lying if I said I wasn't relieved that they're going to discharge you from active duty."

"Prepare to be sick of me."

"I'll let you know when you're overstepping your bounds."

"Sage," he whispered, getting serious again. "Kiss me, darlin'."

I stretched my neck, careful not to jostle the bed as I gave him my lips. The kiss was soft and gentle, nothing like the other ways he'd kissed me before.

My toes didn't curl, but my heart fluttered along with a fresh set of butterflies in my stomach.

"I love you," he murmured against my lips as he stared into my eyes. "Forever and ever."

"Shut up and kiss me again," I said to him, too emotional for words.

He smirked and laughed as his lips came down on mine again, but this time with more force.

"Mine," he breathed into my mouth, and I felt those words, knowing I was his forever.

CHAPTER 22
AUSTIN
THREE MONTHS LATER...

"TOO DAMN LONG SINCE I've laid eyes on that ugly mug." Maverick smacked my back with enough force to knock me off the step before he pulled me into a bear hug. "I thought your ass was never coming back to base."

"I missed you too, asshole," I said to him as I tapped his back to let me go. "You're a sight for sore eyes, old man, but I thought you'd be gone by now."

"Leaving this month. You?"

I slid into the booth as he sat across from me. "They're prepping my papers. Medical."

Maverick nodded. "Figured as much. Where ya headed?"

"Back home."

"And Sage?"

"To her."

"Pensacola sucks dick, man. I'd rather lick a pair

of sweaty balls that haven't been washed in a month than live there."

"Dude, you live where again? Dumbfuck, Nebraska?"

"Still better than Pensacola," he bristled, but he ticked his chin to an area behind me. "The other assholes are here."

I turned with relatively no pain, something I was still getting used to, and saw the other guys from the team. They looked the same. Not much had changed in the short amount of time I'd been in the hospital and rehab, but then again, military life didn't lend itself to change.

"Fucker," Wiz said, staring down at me and surveying my body like he was going to be able to see the damage through my clothes. "You look healthy enough for me to keep your ass here and in the field."

Trig leaned over, looking me over too. "He's always been below average. The wounds will only slow him down more, and then there's his age."

"I'm younger than you, dickhead," I reminded him and turned my gaze toward the bar. "Make your old legs useful and go grab us a bucket of beers."

"Old legs," Trig muttered and gave me the middle finger before he took off toward the crowded bar.

Wizard sat down next to Maverick. "He missed you the most, you know," he said, ticking his head toward the bar and Trigger. "He's torn up over you leaving."

"What am I? Chopped liver?" Maverick asked, touching his chest and doing his best to look hurt by the comment. "Ain't nobody tore up about me leaving too, are they?"

Wizard laughed and then punched Maverick in the arm. "You're an idiot and a whiny little cunt too."

"I'll miss this," I breathed out, stretching my legs under the table as Trigger headed back toward us, looking way too happy to get his hands on a beer.

"Target has been acquired," Trigger said as he set the bucket of twelve beers down in the middle of us. "I've been dying for a cold beer all day."

"I thought you were excited for my company," I teased him, giving Trigger a nudge in the ribs with my elbow.

He didn't even flinch before he grabbed two beers, one for me and one for himself. "I'm fucking happy you're alive, man."

I took the beer from his hands and tipped it to him. "That makes two of us."

"Didn't think you were going to make it," Wizard added as he grabbed his own beer, twisting off the top and dropping the metal on the table. "It was fucked up."

"Ya think?" I said before chugging down half the bottle.

He watched me as I drank, and he continued with the conversation. "Our intel was fucked up, but we got the job done and were able to pull you out."

"Thank fuck for small miracles," I muttered as soon as I swallowed.

"Do you remember anything after you got shot?" Trigger asked.

"Not a damn thing. I remember rounding the structure and then the stars. Next thing I know, I'm waking up in the hospital in Germany, shot to shit and hurting. Then shit gets fuzzy again until I landed my ass in Florida."

I'd thought about that night and the days afterward so many times, but no matter how hard I tried, they were still fuzzy. Images came and went, fading into what felt like a dream.

Maverick scrubbed his hand across his jawline and grimaced. "You were awake when we put your ass on the helo to head back."

"I was? Fuck. I don't have any recollection of that."

Maverick nodded as he lifted the beer bottle to his lips. "Fucked-up shit. You were screaming for Sage. And I'm not talking about yelling, I'm talking about you screaming like a feral beast searching for a part of your body that had fallen off. Never seen anything like it before. Shit was in-fucking-sane."

"My man is in love," Trigger said, bumping me with his shoulder. "It's sweet. He thought he was dying and was screaming out for his girl."

I rolled my eyes. "Shut up, jagoff."

He crossed his arms with his elbows resting on the

table, looking every bit as cool as he always did. "Well, you did, didn't you?"

"I did."

I couldn't deny it anymore. I didn't want to either. I loved Sage. Somehow in this fucked-up world, we worked. Maybe because her dad had lived my life, so she understood more than others. Sprinkle in the fact that she was in the navy too, and we were a match made in heaven.

"You wouldn't move to Pensacola for a piece of ass. That's only for love, man," Maverick stated.

Wizard gaped at me. "Fuckin' Pensacola?"

I nodded. "It's where she's stationed."

"Ugh," Trigger grunted. "Armpit of the state."

"At least my family's not too far."

"Lyndsey wants to move to Florida too," Maverick added. "Maybe we'll end up close by, but it won't be Pensacola."

"The state is big, brother. You could be eight hours away."

"Fuck. Really? It looks like a little thing."

I shook my head. "It doesn't matter. Wherever you are, I'm sure we'll see each other."

There was a sudden heaviness at the table. We'd spent years together. We were a team. A unit. This was the end of an era, something none of us could have ever fathomed, even though it was inevitable. No one stayed in for life, especially not in our specific line of work.

"It's been a wild ride," Wizard said, but there was a sadness to his voice.

"Are you going to sign again?" I asked him.

"Fuck no," he replied quickly, shaking his head. "I'm done after this. I'm not getting my ass killed in some far-off, fucked-up country. I want to retire, get old and fat…"

"You're already both of those things," Trigger said with a tip of his head and beer.

"Fuck you," was Wizard's response. "If you need me, you'll find me on a small island, with my ass on the beach and a beer in my hand."

"You want a buddy there?" Trigger asked. "I got no family and don't know where the hell I'm headed when I get out in a year."

"The beach is big. There's always room for you, buddy."

"You two better find yourself some good women before you get beer guts," Maverick said.

Wizard scoffed. "Women like a thicker man. There's more to hold, fucker."

Maverick barked out a laugh. "That's a crock of shit."

Trigger rubbed his hands together, looking more excited than I'd seen him in a long time. "We'll see. I want a soft woman with lots of curves. Big tits. Big ass. Big hair."

Maverick just shook his head. "You're an idiot."

"That's the dream, Trig," Wizard agreed. "We'll

find that wherever we end up. We'll be beating them off with bats."

"Wherever your asses land, you'd better be careful those women aren't the ones beating you off with bats. You two don't know how to sweet-talk a woman. Never have. Never will."

"Just because you have Lyndsey doesn't mean you're a Romeo, bud. You got lucky," Wizard gave a dramatic pause and took a swig of his beer, "or maybe she's the lucky one since there're not many men who would put up with her bullshit the way you do."

"She's not that bad," Maverick argued, but the man had bitched about Lyndsey for the last four years.

"Does she make you happy?" I asked him.

He nodded. "She does, more than she pisses me off."

"Then, a win is a win, brother," I told him.

"You two dumb fucks are always ragging on my wife, but every night you go to bed with your hand wrapped around your own cock," Maverick told them with a pointed glare. "Until that changes, you can shut the fuck up. Got me?"

"Yeah," Trigger grumbled.

"Whatever," Wizard added.

I chuckled, loving these three fuckers more than I'd ever thought I could love another man who wasn't family.

And although I loved being with them every day, I was ready to be closer to my family and be around Sage all the time. I was over playing G.I. Joe, ready to settle down and live a boring civilian life.

"When do you take off?" Wizard asked me.

"In a few days. Waiting on paperwork."

"Could be months at the pace they move," Maverick added, rolling his eyes. "Does the navy do anything fast?"

"Nope," Trigger clipped. "Not a goddamn thing."

"They've had two months to prepare the shit. They knew I couldn't return to duty after that bullet shattered my leg."

Maverick winced and shivered. "I can't get the image out of my head, man. I had nightmares for weeks."

"It's the end of an era," Wizard said, holding up his beer in the middle of the table. "It was a good run."

We each raised our bottles, clinking them together.

"And we all made it out alive," I added.

That was more than a lot of people who did what we did. We'd left a lot of men behind and told ourselves it was for the greater good, but that didn't make the sting any less painful.

But this was right, and now it was my time to live.

CHAPTER 23
SAGE

"WHAT IN THE..." My voice faded as I gaped at Austin, sitting on the back of a motorcycle, and I was immediately met with a smirk.

"You like it?" He looked so proud of himself, but all I felt was fear.

"No," I snapped, hating the idea of him putting his life in danger.

I didn't know anyone who rode a bike for long and lived to a ripe old age. If the driver wasn't dangerous, the other people in the cars around them were. And Florida wasn't known for the safest drivers in the world either.

He leaned back and ran his hand along the side. "Why not? She's beautiful."

The sun hit him the right way, making his muscles stand out as they rippled. I had to swallow the extra saliva that flooded my mouth at the sight of him on the bike.

Did I like this? Shit. I didn't want to. I really didn't. But damn it, there was something about him on the damn thing that made my belly flutter.

I sighed, hating myself for what I was about to say. "She's okay."

His gaze moved away from his new toy to me. "You want a ride?" he asked, that smirk still firmly planted on his beautiful lips. "Come on. You know you do, darlin'."

"I want a ride, but not on that bike." I smirked back, wishing we were naked and in my bed. "I haven't seen you in weeks."

He used his feet to pull the bike toward me and extended his neck, bringing his face closer to me. "You ride this with me, and then, I'll ride you."

Damn. The way he looked at me and the dirty words coming from his mouth made my knees weak. "You want me to risk my life to sleep with you."

He swept his tongue across his bottom lip, and my eyes followed. "Who's sleeping?"

"Where's Austin? Did he bump his head in California and come back a different man?"

He let out a deep, rich laugh. "Darlin', I'm the same man I was before. I stepped out of the shadow of the military, and I'm ready to live life, with my woman on the back of my bike and nothing but the open road in front of me."

"He clearly hit his head," I whispered to myself.

He reached out, grabbing my hand. "I promise you'll like it."

"That's how I got into this mess in the first place."

He yanked me forward until my body hit his leg. He peered up at me, and every bit of breath and resistance in my body evaporated. "Come on, beautiful. Let your hair down for a while. Let's have some fun."

Before I could reply, his lips were on mine and his arm snaked around me, making it impossible for me to pull away. But I didn't want to stop. It had been far too long since I'd seen him. And the feel of his hard, warm body against mine caused my sense of self-preservation to make a quick exit.

"I'll keep you safe," he said against my lips before pulling away.

I didn't move quickly, but I reluctantly climbed on the back of his bike, letting him help me get positioned.

"Lean forward, put your body against me and your arms around me." He reached down on each side, adjusting my legs onto some pegs.

I did as I was told and didn't hate it. Holding him was never a bad thing. I didn't know if I'd ever sat this close to him without us having sex.

He patted my hands as I slid them to the front of his body. "Hold on, darlin'. I got you. You're safe with me."

I felt that way too. There wasn't another human on the planet whom I'd climb on the back of a bike with, but there was something different about Austin.

"I've been riding since I was a kid. Pike taught me. I'm not new, and I'll go slow."

I trusted his words, swallowing down the fear that crept into my mind as he started the engine. The bike roared to life underneath us, and I instantly felt the power and pull of riding on it.

He drove slowly at first, letting me get used to the feel of the bike underneath me. I didn't like it. It felt too wild, too untamed. There was a motion as if we were skating on glass, and it felt as if he wasn't really in control.

But I pushed that feeling away, letting myself get lost in the feel of his body against mine. I placed my cheek against his back, too petrified to watch the road. My hair drifted behind me, blowing in the wind.

I felt a different kind of peace in all the noise and motion. Something I'd never expected to feel on the back of a motorcycle.

I closed my eyes, losing myself a little and pushing away all thoughts and worries.

It was just him, me, and the wind.

I didn't open my eyes and look up until the bike stopped moving. Austin placed his boot on the ground, and I peered around, confused.

"Where are we?" I asked without moving my body away from his.

"What do you think?"

I blinked, sitting up to get a better look at the adorable little house. "It's..." I soaked it all in. The pale-yellow exterior with flower boxes and a manicured front lawn. And between the houses, I could see the most brilliant blue that could only be the Gulf of Mexico. "It's so damn cute."

"It's mine."

I turned my head toward him, my mouth dropping open. "What?"

He looked over his shoulder at me and smiled. "I wanted a place with a view."

"When?" I asked.

"When what?"

"When did you do this?" I waved my hand toward the house that looked like something out of a fairy tale.

"When I was in rehab. I had a lot of time on my hands. As soon as I saw it, I knew it was right and grabbed it right away." He twisted his body around to me. "You're here for a while, and where you are, I am."

I threw my arms around his neck and hugged him tightly. "I'm so happy you're here." And I meant those words. It hadn't been that long ago we weren't sure if he was going to survive.

"Me too, darlin'. Me too," he whispered as he stared into my eyes. He lifted his hand and dangled a key. "Want to see it?"

I snatched the key ring from his fingers and climbed off the bike like I'd been riding for years. "Yes," I said, taking off toward the door. "Move faster, old man."

He laughed behind me as he unfolded his body from the back of the bike. "I knew you'd like it."

"Like it?" I asked, looking at him over my shoulder for a moment before I jammed the key into the lock. "I freaking love it."

Austin was behind me a second later, his body pressed against me as he placed his hand over mine. "I have big plans for this place," he whispered in my ear as he turned our hands. "I'm going to fuck you in every room."

My breath hitched at his dirty words. "Behave," I whispered, but I rubbed my ass against his denim-covered dick. "You say such filthy things."

"And you fucking love it."

I smirked as he pushed open the door, wanting to feel his hands all over my body. But first, I wanted to see the place he was about to call home.

When the door swung open, my eyes went right to the sliding glass door at the back of the house. It looked more like a picture than reality. The Gulf was the most beautiful shade of blue. The sky seemed to melt into the ocean, shifting color.

Austin came up behind me, wrapping his arms around me as I stood in the middle of the living room. "Do you like it?"

"Yes," I breathed.

"You haven't seen everything."

"The rest doesn't matter when you have that," I said, waving my hand toward the view. "This place had to be a fortune."

"As soon as the person heard that I was a former SEAL, looking to relocate, they gave me the deal of a lifetime. I couldn't say no."

"Job perk."

"It does have its advantages."

I turned in his arms until I could look into his eyes. "I'm happy you're here. My heart is full."

"Darlin'," he whispered, his blue eyes shimmering as he smiled down at me, "I've never felt more alive and filled with possibilities as I do right now."

If I weren't a puddle of goo already, those words would have been enough to send me over the edge.

"I love you, Sage."

"I love you too," I said as I leaned forward, plastering my body against his, and I popped up on my tiptoes to press my mouth against his.

He slid his hands to my ass, lifting me off the floor. I hooked my legs behind his back, securing myself to him, and murmured, "Fuck me, baby."

A low, deep growl vibrated through him as he carried me toward the bedroom in a frenzy of lips and tongues. As soon as my feet landed on the bedroom floor, we yanked at each other's clothes, unable to get naked fast enough.

I tore my mouth away from his, panting. "Condom," I gasped, hungry and impatient for him to be inside me.

He turned around, giving me a great view of his bare ass, and rooted around in a dresser drawer. When he faced me again, condom in hand, the joy on his face was like he was holding a prize at a carnival. But I didn't have long to appreciate his handsome features so filled with excitement because his lips were on mine a second later.

He worked the wrapper of the condom as his tongue tangled with mine. And when he nudged me onto the bed, covering me with his body as soon as my back touched the comforter, there was no more time to wait.

He slid inside me slowly, never pulling his mouth away from mine. Our bodies moved in rhythm, rocking back and forth, him stuffing me completely.

It didn't take long for my body to tighten as the orgasm built until I couldn't stop the waves of pleasure from crashing over me.

CHAPTER 24
AUSTIN

"ARE YOU EXCITED TO SEE EVERYONE?" Sage asked as we walked up the driveway at my grandparents' house.

I squeezed her hand and smiled. "I'm always happy to come home."

Although I hadn't started out with this group as my family, they were everything I had now, besides Sage. Lucky for me, my brother married into something great. They welcomed me with open arms, and from the moment I moved to Florida, they made me feel like I'd always belonged there.

But before I could touch the handle, the door opened. "Austin," my grandmother said, holding her arms out to me. "I've missed you."

"Gram," I said, walking into her embrace but keeping my hand in Sage's. "You just saw me a few months ago."

They'd visited me in the hospital in Gainesville. The entire family had. If I'd had any doubt in my mind if I was a member of the Gallo family, my hospital stay wiped it completely away.

She kissed my cheek lightly as she damn near squeezed the life out of me. "Months," she mumbled. "Too long. Too long."

When she released me, her gaze immediately fell on Sage. "It's so good to see you, dear. I hope you brought that appetite of yours with you."

Sage giggled. "Of course I did, Mrs. G."

Gram motioned for Sage to give her a hug. "You get one too," she said to her.

Sage gazed at me like I'd had any role in this happening. Gram always did what she wanted, and that included giving love to every single person who walked into her house. I gave Sage a chin lift before her feet became unstuck from the cement porch.

Sage practically ran into my gram's arms.

"Austin!" Joe yelled from somewhere inside the house. "Get your ass in here."

"I'm being summoned," I said, walking around Gram and Sage as they hugged on the porch.

I marched into the house to find Joe standing in the foyer with his wife, Suzy. They were the closest thing I had to parents, even though they were Gigi's. "Hey, kid. It's good to see you up and walking around," Joe said, giving me a rare smile. "Never thought I'd see the day."

I laughed, shaking my head. "Me neither. Thought I was a goner there for a bit."

"Life wouldn't be the same without you here with the rest of the family."

Hearing those words from him felt good. "Thanks, Joe."

"Need anything?" Suzy asked, her eyes moving down my body to my legs, where I'd sustained the majority of the damage.

"A new body."

She gave me a sorrowful smile. "Can't help you there, kiddo. But if I could, I would."

"Austin, is that you? Come back here!" Gigi yelled from somewhere in the back of the house. "And Sage better be with you."

Sage stepped into the house as if she'd heard the call. "Hey," she said, tucking her hair behind her ear.

Grandma Gallo was right behind her. "Dinner will be ready in an hour."

"Got it, Ma," Suzy said to her as she walked toward the kitchen. "You want help?"

"No, baby. You rest."

Suzy shrugged. "I'd do more damage than good."

"You've gotten better, Sunshine," Joe said to his wife, giving her a squeeze.

"Or maybe your taste buds have adjusted to the mediocrity."

He leaned over and kissed the top of her head. "Possible," he muttered against her hair.

"They're so cute," Sage whispered as she took my hand in hers. "I want that."

"Me too," I whispered back.

I'd lied to myself for a long time, pretending I didn't want a relationship. I'd told myself that they weren't for me. But that was because I hadn't met the right person.

But things in my mind had shifted over the last year. Sage had done that for me—or was it *to* me? She'd made me see how my life could be if I allowed myself to dream bigger.

"Come find us after dinner, Austin. We want to talk to you about something," Joe said.

"Sure thing, Joe," I replied because there wasn't anything I wouldn't do for the man.

Gigi rounded the corner of the foyer and placed her hands on her hips. "You have a hearing problem from too much pew pew?"

I jerked my head back, wondering what in the hell she was talking about. "Too much pew pew?"

She rolled her eyes before explaining, outstretching two fingers like a gun. "Gunshots, bud. I called for you to come back there."

"I only move so fast, babe." I tapped my hip. "Body does what it wants."

She stared at me, knowing full well I was making an excuse for not moving my ass fast enough. "Sorry," she said, not wanting to appear to be insensitive. "You guys done here?" Her gaze slid to her parents for a second before coming back to Sage and me.

"We're done. Lead the way, sis," I told Gigi, wrapping my arm around Sage's back.

Her demeanor instantly changed. "It's been forever since you've joined us on the patio. We're a little overly excited. Sorry about that, Austin," Gigi said as we walked through the house.

"Austin!" the family yelled out as soon as I walked into the big, open space at the back of the house. It was where the kitchen was and the family room, overlooking the pool. That was the perfect name too. It wasn't a living room, but the place the older people in the family hung out every Sunday.

"Us first," Gigi told them, ignoring their calls for me to come see them.

I shrugged. "The boss has spoken. I'll be back," I told them, not letting my steps falter.

"She's a bossy thing," Aunt Fran said, shaking her head in disbelief. "Been months, and she's hogging that man all to herself. Hey, Sage. You're a sight for sore eyes."

"Hey," Sage said back with a wave and the biggest smile on her face.

Pike was waiting for us just outside the sliding glass doors. I barely got both feet on the cement before he grabbed me. "I missed you, fucker," he said as he wrapped me in an almost bone-crunching hug.

I barely noticed as Gigi ushered Sage away from me for her to go talk to the girls.

"I missed you too, asshole," I told him, letting him hug me longer than normal. "I'm glad to be back."

I'd gone for long stretches without being here, but that had been on my own terms. My own decision. But not physically being able to come here because of an injury had made me miserable.

Sure, they'd brought me food to reheat in the hospital microwave, but it wasn't the same. I wasn't surrounded by my people...my family.

"Let the man go," Mammoth said to my brother when the hug went on for a ridiculous amount of time. "You need to share him. Don't be a hog."

"Exactly," Tamara said as she pushed back her hair and stalked my way. She practically peeled my brother away from me. "I know he's your brother, but we all missed him."

There was no doubt in my mind that these were my people. When I was a teenager and moved here, I wasn't sure I'd ever feel like a member of the family, but now I knew I belonged here. I was one of them.

Tamara gripped my shoulder, hip checking my brother out of the way. "You look—" her gaze skated down my body "—back in one piece."

"Not quite good as new," I told her with a soft smile.

"I'm sure you could still beat any of their old

asses, though. Even on one leg." She giggled as some of the guys grumbled.

"And an arm tied behind my back," I teased them.

Tamara kept laughing as she wrapped herself around me. "I did miss you, Austin. It's good to have you in the same state again."

"You just miss having a partner in crime. No one else talks more shit than me, except you."

My body shook as she chuckled. "You say such sweet things." When she released me, she turned toward Sage and the other girls. "You going to marry her?"

"I think so."

Tamara bumped me with her shoulder. "That wasn't very convincing, Austin. I always thought you were smart, but if you don't, you're the world's biggest idiot."

"I have to find the right time."

"Life isn't perfect. The time doesn't matter as much as the words and what you do afterward."

I stared at Tamara's profile, noticing the smallest crinkles near her eyes. "You mean like asking her and then banging her?"

Tamara bent her neck to stare at the cement. "God, you're such a freaking moron. Men," she muttered before lifting her head and narrowing her eyes at me. "I meant how you treat her while you're married. Doesn't matter if you have the most romantic engagement story if you're an asshole after you say your vows."

"I'll treat her like a queen," I told her.

"Queen in the streets, hooker in the sheets." She nudged me again, laughing. "Don't forget that."

"I swear to fuck, you should've been a dude."

"The world couldn't handle all this if I had a dick between my legs."

I gave her a chin lift and held in my laughter. "No truer words have ever been spoken."

"You better lock her ass down," Mammoth whispered in my ear as he walked by, headed toward the slider, and he disappeared inside.

"He's bossy."

Tamara smiled. "That's what I love most about him."

My eyebrows furrowed. "Really?"

"Fuck no," she blurted out. "It's his monster cock."

I threw up my hands and stalked away. "Damn it. I walked right into that one."

"Dummy," Tamara called out as I walked across the lanai to where Sage was with the other girls.

"Hey, baby," I said, wrapping my arm around her waist again. "Are they treating you right?"

Lily smacked my stomach with her hand from her seat. "Don't be ridiculous. Of course we are. She's one of us now."

"It's finally an even split."

I rolled my eyes. For years, the women in the family had been going on and on about how the number of women versus men had been out of balance because I was the last holdout. But now, with Sage here, they were seeing their numbers finally shift toward equality.

"I don't think…" Sage started.

Rebel held up her hand. "No. You are. There's no question about it. Right, girls?" she asked the others.

They nodded in unison.

"Unless Austin fucks it up," Olive said, giving me a judgmental stare.

"Not fucking anything up."

Sage plastered herself against me as she hugged my waist. "He's a good guy."

The women all laughed like it was the most ludicrous thing they'd ever heard.

"He may be now, but he wasn't always," Arlo said, crossing her arms in front of her chest.

I couldn't even argue with her. I used to be a total asshole, and I didn't give a shit about anyone's feelings except my own.

"We all have our pasts," Sage said, hugging me tightly as she peered up at me. "Only thing that matters is the future."

Butterflies filled me as she looked up at me. There wasn't a doubt in my mind that I had found my forever, and that scared the living shit out of me.

CHAPTER 25
SAGE

"WILL you and Uncle Austin play water balloons with us?" Gigi and Pike's little girl Maria asked, twisting her curls on the end of her finger. She looked so innocent, but in my limited experience with this family, none of them were.

"Oh, I don't know," I told her as I looked around for Austin, but I didn't see him anywhere. "I can ask him."

She gave me an impish smile. "I promise it'll be fun."

I playfully tugged on the bottom of her sundress. "You promise to go easy on me?"

She twisted her body back and forth, her smile never wavering. "I promise you won't get too wet." I saw a twinkle in her eyes that meant there was nothing but trouble ahead for me.

"I'll go ask him."

"Harley and Salvatore are getting the balloons ready," she explained. "Tons and tons of balloons." Her little body practically vibrated with excitement as she told me all the details.

"I'll go ask Austin," I said as I pushed myself off the lounge chair near the pool.

It was good I got up. If I'd lain there any longer, I most certainly would've fallen asleep. I had a belly filled with too much pasta and everything else that his grandmother had put on my plate, whether I wanted it or not.

I walked into the kitchen, and Fran pointed toward the dining room as soon as she saw me. Everyone in the family seemed to know what everyone else thought or needed.

My feet came to a screeching halt as I stepped into the dining room. Joe and Suzy were sitting at the dining room table with Austin.

"Sorry," I said, ducking my head, ready to turn around to leave them alone.

They looked like they were talking about something serious and none of my business.

"No. Wait," Austin said as he reached over and pulled out the chair next to him. "Stay."

"It's okay, sweetheart," Suzy said as she folded her hands on top of the table.

My gaze moved around to the three of them, wondering if they were only being kind. I walked slowly, as if the floor was made of glass. "I don't want to interrupt or intrude."

Austin lifted his hand and latched on to my wrist as soon as I was close enough. "Darlin', you're my girl, and there's nothing that can't be said in front of you. I want you here."

"Oh," I mumbled as I took the seat next to him. "Is something wrong?" I looked from Austin to Joe.

I was met with a headshake from Joe. "Nothing's wrong."

"Then what's up?" Austin asked Joe as he held my hand underneath the table. "I feel like you pulled me in here because I'm in trouble."

Suzy giggled and waved Austin off. "You're a grown man who's been busy saving the world. I hardly think there's anything you could do that would get you in trouble with us."

Joe scrubbed his beard with his hand. "Suzy and I have been talking," he started and then stopped to blow out a breath before continuing. "We may be way off base and out of place with this conversation, but…"

"We want to adopt you," Suzy blurted out.

My eyes widened at her words. Adoption? Austin was a little old for that, but weirder things had happened.

"You want to adopt me?" Austin asked, speaking slowly, like he didn't believe the words that were coming out of his mouth.

The squeeze of my hand underneath the table told me that he really didn't believe what he was hearing. But I couldn't tell what he thought about the proposition.

Suzy nodded. "I may not have given birth to you, but I think of you as my own. You've been part of our family since the day you walked in the door. When the accident happened, I was beside myself."

"That's putting it mildly," Joe muttered.

Suzy swatted his hand but carried on without missing a beat. "You're one of us and deserve a permanent place here. Joe and I would be honored if you'd allow us to adopt you so there's never a doubt about where you belong."

"You want to adopt me?" Austin whispered again, blinking rapidly like there was something in his eyes.

Joe nodded this time. "I always wanted a son. Don't get me wrong. I love my girls more than the air I breathe, but I'd be honored if you'd be willing to be my son."

I stared at Austin, wondering how he'd reply to something like this. If I were in his shoes, I wasn't sure what I'd say.

"We love you, Austin" Suzy added. "But it's totally okay if you say no. We won't be hurt. We'll understand. If you need time to think about…"

"No," Austin blurted out.

Suzy's face fell. "No?"

Austin shook his head and squeezed my hand

again. "No. I mean, yes. Yes, I want that. I want to be your kid."

My eyes started to sting as tears pricked at them. This moment was heavy and sweet.

"I wish I had always been your kid. Maybe my life would've been different," he said. "Maybe I could've been a better man."

Joe smiled at Austin and blew out a long breath through his mouth. "You're a good man, Austin. You did amazing things. Things most people could only dream of. Changing one thing in your journey would put you on a different course. I'm proud of the man you are and have become, and it's going to be wonderful to watch you grow more as you become a husband and father to my future grandchildren."

My belly flipped at the thought of children—Joe and Suzy's future grandchildren. Would they be mine? I wanted that. I wanted a family. I wanted a future as part of this family too. They were the most wonderful group of people. I loved Austin, and I loved his entire family too. I could never imagine walking away.

Suzy pushed herself up from the table and came around to where Austin and I were sitting. She leaned over and wrapped her arms around his neck, kissing his cheek. "You've made me the happiest woman in the world today."

He patted her hands that rested near his

collarbone. "No, Suzy, you made me the happiest man."

"Someday, when you feel ready, you can call me Ma."

"Ma," he whispered, melting into her embrace. "I love that."

I looked in Joe's direction, and there was nothing except pure joy on his face. He looked more content than he had when we'd walked in the door earlier. I was sure this conversation had been weighing on his mind, along with the possibility that Austin would say no.

Austin looked across the table at Joe. "Can I call you my old man?"

"Not if you want to keep breathing," Joe answered, but he immediately smiled. "But then again, you know more than a few moves to put me on my ass, so there's not much I could do about it if you did."

"Only a few moves?" Austin asked.

"I never tangled with a SEAL. I don't know what you can do, but at my age, I'm not willing to find out either."

They had an easy relationship. I'd seen the banter more than once, and it was always filled with love. Sitting there, listening to them, made me miss my family...even Sawyer.

"You two need to stop," Suzy warned them. "Not even a little play fighting."

"Are you worried I'll get hurt?" Austin asked her.

She shook her head. "I'm worried my old man will need a cane or a full-body cast afterward. The man doesn't have an off switch."

"Jesus," Joe muttered.

Suzy straightened and placed her hands on Austin's shoulders. "Should we tell everyone the news?" She glanced down. "Is that okay, Austin?"

"Hell yeah. Tell everyone. Do Pike or Gigi know?"

"No, baby," Suzy answered, still standing behind him. "I didn't want to tell anyone on the chance you'd say no, but I know they'll be happy."

"Let's find out." Austin released my hand, pushed back his chair, and stood as Suzy backed up. He turned to face her and opened his arms. "But first, I want a real hug."

Suzy's smile widened as she moved into his arms and wrapped herself around him. "You made me so happy, kid."

"No, Ma. You made me the happiest person in the world. It's nice to know I'm not alone in this world."

"You've never been alone, Austin. We've always been here for you, even when you weren't around. But we're your home, and life isn't the same when you're not around."

Damn it. The tears that had somehow managed to stay in my eyes started to trickle out. My makeup was going to be a mess. I knew better than to wear mascara that wasn't waterproof. I patted under my eyes, trying to save my makeup from further devastation.

"Come on. We better get out there. People are going to start to get worried," Joe said as he got up from the table.

Austin and Suzy peeled away from each other, but before Joe could leave the room, Austin marched up to him and wrapped his arms around the man. Within a second, Joe's feet were off the floor.

"I freakin' love you, man," Austin said to him as Joe gave in to Austin's strength.

"Okay. Okay. Put me down, kid. I get it. You're stronger."

Austin set Joe back on the floor, and as soon as his feet touched the wood floor, he pulled Austin in for a real hug. "I love you, bud, but don't do that shit again."

Austin pulled his head back. "You that breakable?"

Joe narrowed his eyes. "I don't want to find out. Do you?"

Austin chuckled as they let each other go. "I'd never hurt my dad."

A look passed between the two of them. So many emotions went through me as I watched two grown men show their love for each other.

"Fuck," Joe mumbled, wiping at his eyes.

"Come on. Come on," Suzy said, waving her hands for us to follow her.

As soon as I stood up, Austin held out his hand for me. "You okay?" he asked.

I nodded but didn't speak. I didn't trust my voice just yet and worried talking would open the floodgates that I tried so hard to keep a hold on.

We followed Joe and Suzy as they walked out of the dining room. As soon as we entered the kitchen, Suzy cleared her throat, and when the talking didn't die down, Joe whistled to get everyone's attention.

"We have an announcement to make," Suzy said when everyone was quiet, and all eyes were on us. "Joe and I are proud to announce, we're having a boy."

CHAPTER 26
AUSTIN

SIX MONTHS LATER...

SAGE ROLLED against my chest before her body had a chance to go limp. "That was…" she gasped, trying to catch her breath.

My fingers traced a path back and forth along her arm. "Yeah," I whispered as my heart thudded underneath her head. "I swear you're trying to kill me."

She giggled and snuggled closer to me. "I figured you could take it. I didn't hear you complain when I was riding you, baby."

I lifted her hand to my mouth and smirked as I brushed my lips against her skin. "A man would rather die in the act than do anything that'll make a woman stop. If I go out with you sliding up and down on my cock, I'll die a happy man."

She peered up at me in amazement. "Can you imagine?"

"It would be an awkward conversation for you, but I wouldn't care because I'd be dead."

"Sir," she said, using her best cop voice, "what were you two doing when he stopped breathing?" She stopped talking and started to laugh. "How horrifying."

"I promise not to go out that way. I wouldn't want you to be horrified about how *I* died."

"You're not allowed."

"Not allowed to what?"

"Die," she whispered.

"Darlin', everyone dies eventually."

"Not until you're really, really old and I am too. I want a lifetime with you before that happens."

For months, I'd been planning to ask Sage to marry me. None of the ways I'd dreamed up felt right. But right then, in that moment, the timing was perfect.

I rolled over, moving Sage under me. I stared down at her, searching her eyes. "I want a lifetime with you too, Sage. I'm not sure that will be long enough, even if we have a hundred years together. Marry me, Sage. Let's start that future right now. I want you to be my wife."

Her mouth dropped open. "Are you asking me to marry you while you're naked on top of me?"

I smiled as I settled my body between her legs. "Yep. And your answer is?" God, she was killing me here. Her answering my question with another question wasn't a good sign.

Maybe I'd read everything wrong. Maybe she was the type who never wanted to get married. Maybe she wasn't about conforming to societal norms. She was all about girl power, and I loved that about her too.

She lifted her arms and wrapped them around my shoulders. "Yes, Austin, I'll marry you. There's nothing more that I want in this world than to be your wife and carry your babies."

"You want to carry my babies? Like, more than one?" I whispered, a smidge of fear blocking my throat.

I'd never put much thought into having kids. It wasn't like I had the best parents or the greatest childhood. I wouldn't bring a baby into a world where they would have the same issues to deal with. But I wasn't in the military anymore. I wasn't putting my life at risk on a daily basis. I'd done my duty, and civilian life was less dangerous—but not completely danger-free.

"At least two, but I'd love three or five."

My mouth went dry. "Five?" My stomach twisted at the thought of five little humans running around our house, screaming their heads off and fighting.

Sage reached up, cupping my cheeks. "I want what the Gallos have. I want to grow old and be surrounded by generations of our own."

I loved the sound of that. After feeling alone for so

many years, especially after Pike left home, I craved nothing more than being in the company of people who loved me. I had that with the Gallos, but the idea of having that with my own family made my heart flutter.

"We'll have as many as you want."

"Good," she said, smiling up at me. "Smart man."

"Whatever will make you happy. When do you want to start?" I placed a kiss on her nose.

"Soon. You're not getting any younger." She giggled softly until I nudged her with my cock.

"Hey now. This thing has a lot of years left in it."

She reached down between us, fisting my dick in her soft, warm hands. "I want to be your wife before I get pregnant."

"I can make that happen this weekend."

"You're so romantic."

"We can elope to Vegas."

"No, Austin. I want our families to be with us on that day. My parents would never forgive me if I ran off and got married without them being there with us."

"I don't think mine would either," I told her, thinking about Suzy and Joe and how they were officially my parents now. We'd signed the adoption paperwork and went before a judge two months ago.

I still couldn't believe it was real. To say I was shocked when they asked me if they could adopt me was an understatement. Never in a million years could I have imagined they'd want to become my parents.

They'd welcomed me into the family since the first day I'd moved in with Gigi and Pike. And I hadn't been all that likable back then. I'd had a lot of anger about the death of my mother and my father being a total and complete shithead. But that didn't stop them from being kind and understanding.

If I could've picked my parents before I was born, I would've picked a couple like Joe and Suzy. They were good people—no, they were the best.

Sage tapped my cheek. "Hey, where did you go there?"

I blinked, pushing away the thoughts of the past. "Thinking about how fast life can change."

Her palm cupped my face. "Good or bad?"

"In my life...both, but recently, everything has changed for the better, and I want it to stay that way."

"It is going to stay that way too," she said, promising something neither of us had any control over.

EPILOGUE

SAGE

Three years later…

"GIVE ME THAT LITTLE PUMPKIN," Suzy said as soon as we walked through the front door.

I didn't even have a chance to take off my shoes before she had Maggie out of my arms and in hers.

"You're absolutely perfect," Suzy whispered as she touched Maggie's cheek. "Your grandma loves you."

Tears pricked my eyes, something that had become the norm since I'd become pregnant. The hormones had wreaked havoc on me and didn't stop after I gave birth.

"Darlin'," Austin whispered in my ear as he ushered me through the foyer. "You okay?"

"I'm happy," I told him, wiping my eyes. "So happy."

Austin pulled me against his side. "Maybe this was too much, too soon."

I shook my head and sniffled. "No, this is perfect. I've missed this."

We'd spent two months in the house, trying to limit Maggie's exposure to large crowds. It was a bit overkill, but as new parents, we were panicked about damn near everything, including germs, until her immune system had a chance to develop more.

"Me too," he said as he looped his arm around my back and moved me toward the rear of the house. "I heard Gram is making all our favorites."

I snorted. "Everything she makes is my favorite."

The woman didn't miss. Every dish she prepared was something I could eat on a daily basis and never get tired of either.

"Baby," Grandma Gallo said, rushing toward me instead of the baby. "Come sit down. I need to feed you."

I smiled as she grabbed my arm, ushering me toward a barstool in her kitchen and away from Austin.

"You need food to have enough energy for that little bundle of joy."

"Austin's been keeping me well-fed. I'm not starving."

She stared at me for a few seconds before she made her way around the other side of the island. "Is he a good cook?"

"Decent."

"I'll send you home with all the leftovers."

"There's our girl," Fran said, wrapping an arm around me. "You look good, mama. Motherhood suits you."

"If by looking good, you mean feeling like shit, then it does."

Fran pulled herself up on the stool next to me, turning to look at my profile. "Nope. Still as pretty as ever. You want some help at home? Mar and I can come over a few nights a week to give you a break."

I shook my head, loving them for asking, but hating to put them out. "No. We're okay. I'll sleep again someday."

"You'll never get another good night's rest again. It's what it's like being a parent. There will always be worry. Sometimes less. Sometimes more. But it'll always be there. You learn to function on less sleep."

"I thought the military trained me to function on only a few hours, but I wasn't prepared for her."

Fran patted my arm as Grandma plated some food for me. "You just do the best you can," Fran said. "But we're still going to come help. It's what family does, sweetheart."

"That's really sweet, but you two have lives to live."

Fran and Grandma both laughed, but this time, Grandma was the one to reply. "Honey, we lived our lives. Did all the things we wanted to do. Now, we're here to be with our family, help them when necessary, and that includes you, Austin, and little Maggie. We'll come over once a week so you can take a long bath, have a nap, or do whatever you want. Go on a date with your husband, maybe."

All of that sounded so great, and I appreciated them more than I could ever fully express to them.

"And the bonus is baby kisses," Fran added. "There's nothing like snuggling a little one. They grow up far too fast."

I sighed. "I know. While time often seems to move at a snail's pace, I just look at her and see her growing before my very eyes."

Grandma slid a plate of meatballs and eggplant Parmesan in front of me. "It's bittersweet, baby. We understand. Time passes too quickly, especially at our ages."

"There never seems to be enough, does there?" I asked them, wanting their life wisdom.

I never knew my grandparents, but I wished I had. It was why I loved being around the Gallos. They offered so much wisdom, knowledge that could only be gained through years of experience.

"I wish we could live forever. I can't imagine not being around for my children, grandchildren, and great-grandchildren someday. But as with everything else, they'll go on without me."

Fran waved her hand at Grandma. "Bitch, you better not die before me. Do not leave me here with all these old, cranky men. If that happens, I'm jumping in your grave with you."

"The men won't last long with your cooking, Fran," Grandma said back to her, "but don't you dare jump in my grave and cause a scene. I know you love attention, but that's not the way to get it. Let me die and be buried in peace."

My heart ached as they talked, imagining life without them. It didn't seem possible, even if I knew, someday, we'd all take our last breaths. I was lost in my feelings, deciding to dig into the plate in front of me instead of crying.

"I don't think Bear could live without you."

Fran rolled her eyes. "That man could survive a nuclear strike. I mean, my cooking hasn't killed him, so I think he's pretty much like a cockroach. He'll go on even after the world ends."

"I'll what?" Bear asked as he walked into the room as if he were summoned.

As soon as he was behind Fran's stool, she rested her head on his chest. "I'm talking about how you're unstoppable."

"Baby, I'm many things, but unstoppable isn't one of them. We all have our weaknesses, and mine is you." He bent down, kissing her forehead. "You're my world."

My insides turned to mush at the way they loved each other. It was hard to imagine they hadn't been together for their entire lives because they loved each other so hard and so completely.

"I told Mar she can't go before me."

His brows furrowed as he gazed between the two women. "Go where?"

"If she dies before me," Fran explained, like they were having a casual conversation about going to the grocery store and not the final trip we'll all eventually take.

Bear staggered backward like someone had sucker-punched him, but his hands never left the back of her stool. "You're not dying on me...never happening."

"You guys are grim, man," Austin said as he sauntered into the kitchen. "No more death talk. This is a happy day, and I'm not going to let you ruin it talking about your mortality, which is something you guys have become more obsessed with as the years have passed."

"You'll understand when you're closer to the grave than the cradle," Fran told him.

"No one knows how close they are. Hell, you guys almost outlived me." He pointed down at his leg that had been injured, and while it had been repaired, it would never be the same.

Every time he got undressed in front of me, I was reminded of that horrible time when I'd thought I'd lose him.

"Fine. Fine," Grandma said, lifting her hands in defeat. "We're all going to live forever. Happy now?"

"Thank you." Austin cracked a smile. "Let me live in that fantasy for a while longer."

"I'm with him," I said, but my words came out garbled because I'd chosen to jam half a meatball in my mouth while he was speaking.

If I could make one wish, it would be for this moment, surrounded by our entire family, to last forever. A life without the Gallos would be no life at all.

MEN OF INKED CHICAGO #1

When Tate Gallo turned thirty, she swore off three things—drinking, donuts, and dating.

Giving up drinking and dating were easy, but donuts…almost impossible.

But then a handsome man with a wicked grin, hungry eyes, and an interesting proposition makes her question her decision.

Crave releases April 2, 2024
PREORDER CRAVE HERE!
or visit *menofinked.com/crave*

LOVE SIGNED PAPERBACKS?

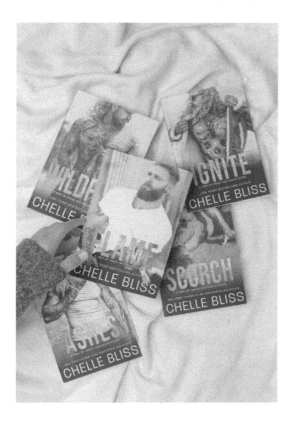

Visit *chelleblissromance.com* for signed paperbacks and
book merchandise.

NEED MORE MEN OF INKED?

Have you read the Men of Inked Southside series?
Visit ***menofinked.com/southside*** to learn more
and be prepared for the Men of Inked Chicago, the
next generation, coming Spring 2024!

Book 1 - Broken Sparrow (Morris)
Book 2 - Broken Dove (Leo)
Book 3 - Broken Wings (Crow)
Book 4 - Broken Arrow (Arrow)

To learn more, please visit
menofinked.com/open-road-series

WANT SIGNED PAPERBACKS?

Visit *chelleblissromance.com* for signed paperbacks and
book merchandise.

MEN OF INKED
FAMILY TREE

MENOFINKED.COM/BOOKS

Check out a bigger version at ***menofinked.com/
gallo-family-tree*** or view the series reading order at
menofinked.com/gallo-saga

**Want to be the first to know about the next
Men of Inked?** Join my newsletter by tapping here
to sign up or visit *menofinked.com/inked-news*

Want a place to talk romance books, meet other bookworms, and all things Men of Inked? Join Chelle Bliss Books on Facebook to get sneak peeks, exclusive news, and special giveaways.

"**Beautiful. Poignant**. This book will stay with you long after you've finished." ~ *Rachel Van Dyken, #1 NYT bestselling author*

"An **emotional journey** you won't soon forget." ~ *Meredith Wild, #1 NYT bestselling author*

Tap here to learn more about Enshrine or visit *menofinked.com/enshrine* for more info.

ABOUT THE AUTHOR

I'm a full-time writer, time-waster extraordinaire, social media addict, coffee fiend, and ex-history teacher. *To learn more about my books, please visit menofinked.com.*

Want to stay up-to-date on the newest
Men of Inked release and more?
Join my newsletter at *menofinked.com/news*

Join over 10,000 readers on Facebook in Chelle Bliss Books private reader group and talk books and all things reading. Come be part of the family!

Where to Follow Me:

facebook.com/authorchellebliss1

instagram.com/authorchellebliss

bookbub.com/authors/chelle-bliss

goodreads.com/chellebliss

tiktok.com/@chelleblissauthor

amazon.com/author/chellebliss

x.com/ChelleBliss1

pinterest.com/chellebliss10

Printed in the USA
CPSIA information can be obtained
at www.ICGtesting.com
LVHW032024020224
770793LV00040B/1115

9 781637 434024